THE COWGIRL TAKES THE BOUNTY

COWGIRL MYSTERIES BOOK 2

SUSAN LOWER

Cover by Beck and Dot

978-1-945274-07-7

In Apple Pie Order...

THE COWGIRL TAKES THE BOUNTY

It's Thursday night, and the table is set for a dinner party inside the dining room of the Deadwood Hotel. Outside, the rain comes down, slow and steady. I watched the stage unload its passengers and head for the stables earlier in the day. Whoever planned on leaving tonight will have to stay until the rain lets up.

Inside, a fire crackles to ward off the chill. It's early May, and I can't seem to shake this foreboding chill.

Daphne Davenport pushes back one of her dark curls, narrowing her almost violet eyes at a waitress handing Pierce Weston, aka the gambler, a drink.

A few weeks ago, the gambler won my hand in marriage in a card game along with half the rights to my father and I's claim up in the mountains.

While he might have gotten my father's half of the claim, thanks to the bounty hunter's quick thinking and a judge, he didn't get me.

The gambler lifts his brandy glass, swirling it before taking a sip. He's a sly one, this gambling man. I wouldn't put anything past him. Even now, his eyes, emerald, like the jewel, take in everyone in the room. His gaze lingers on me for the longest.

Even though Daphne has made it clear, the gambler is hers. I still have something he wants. Without the other half of the claim, he can't sell it to the railroad and make a fortune. I can't afford to let him. There is more at stake than money. An entire tribe of people depends on the land.

The gambler winks and Daphne reaches for her fan from the corner of the table, snapping it open and hiding half her face.

Her eastern frills haven't gone unnoticed. Jed Warner, the hotel owner, can't keep his eyes off her.

Daphne is the daughter of Mr. Davenport, an investor from Boston who has traveled west with Thomas Conway, who owns the railroad coming through Deadwood.

"Jo-Dee!" Daphne Davenport turns her attention to me. Ever since we met a couple weeks back, she has gotten my name wrong. Hearing Jo Dean, she took it for Jo-Dee.

I'm still getting used to the fact that it isn't my name anymore. It's not Dean. It's Townes. That's right, Mrs. Chord Townes. I'm married to the bounty hunter.

I met him the day my father died. Right after good ole Earl bet me and our mine claim on a card game. He lost. The gambler won. And my father turned up dead.

"Daphne." I grit my teeth and try to smile. She's got her hair twisted up in the back, much like I imagine her panties are over the gambler.

"I hear congratulations are in order." She opens her arms and gives me the biggest hug. I stand, arms down. It takes a moment before I can gently pat her on the back. Then she's two steps away, her attention on the gambler. "That was sly of you."

"I don't know what you're talking about."

"Oh, please." She giggles, covering her mouth with that fan

of hers and batting her lashes. Is she trying to flirt with the gambler this far away? Her high-pitched giggle catches the attention of two gentlemen speaking with Daphne's father, Mr. Davenport. I've never seen these men before tonight.

One wears a brown jacket and bolo around his neck. He's not bad to look at. The other has jet black hair and a hawk-like nose. He nods at Daphne, but her eyes are on the gambler's back.

"Miss Davenport," the bounty hunter comes to stand beside me.

"Mr. Townes," Daphne says, "I was telling your wife how happy I am for the two of you."

The bounty hunter lifts a brow in my direction. He's not much for words. It's not the first time someone has congratulated us since news of our union hit the town paper.

The Deadwood News dedicated most of the paper this week to the story of the capture of my father's killer and my marriage.

When I think things are going to get awkward, Mr. Davenport approaches, motioning for Daphne to come his way. "I believe dinner will be served shortly."

"Isn't it so nice of Mr. Warner to host tonight's gathering?" she asks.

"Would you like to come with me to thank him?"

I know on good authority Jed Warner, the hotel owner, has his eyes set on Daphne.

"I don't believe I see him. I should stay here with Daddy and the others. After all, I'm not married like you are. It wouldn't be proper for me to go out alone." Her painted pink lips curl in a devious smile.

I spot the gambler. He's been keeping his distance by the fireplace.

Along with him stands the man with black hair. They're deep in conversation. Whatever the gambler has said, the black-haired guy doesn't like it. He shakes his head, and the gambler's face hardens.

"Jo?" The bounty hunter stands beside me. For a moment, I stare at him. He's wearing a dark navy shirt, and his hair hangs below his shoulders.

He hung his long leather jacket on the wall when we first came in. Sherman, the hotel's clerk, assured him with his life, no one would mess with it. The bounty hunter wears his six-shooter against this thigh. He has a habit of keeping on hand rested on the handle. His free hand touches the small of my back. It's a pure jolt of warmth going up my spine.

"Who's that man?" I ask.

"Which one?"

"Either of them."

The bounty hunter leans close to me. I soak up his warmth in the chilled room. I noticed all the wooden tables and chairs have recently been polished. The room smells of beeswax and pig fat. Even the chandeliers sparkle.

Warner has gone out of his way to impress us tonight. I chalk it up to the railroad gurus coming into town.

I wore my green dress again tonight, the one the bounty hunter bought for me. This time, Ruby helped me with the corset. She doesn't pull as hard as the bounty hunter. Besides, the last time the bounty hunter pulled on my ties, it was downright illegal.

Judge Stevens married us with the bang of his gavel. No vows or pretty words. No kiss to seal the deal. Just BAM! I become Mrs. Chord Townes.

"He works for Conway."

"Who?"

"Gilbert Harris. Are you paying attention or too busy eyeballing Weston?" He says it as if the thought might annoy him. The bounty hunter couldn't possibly be jealous, could he? I tuck the thought away for later.

"The one with the black hair?"

"Lloyd Coose." the bounty hunter's breath tickles my ear. It might look as though we're having an intimate moment to anyone observing us.

"There's something about him," I mutter, more to myself than the bounty hunter.

"He's a scout. According to Conway, he's the man who goes ahead of the crew laying track and finds the best route, reports back to Conway to secure the land."

"Too bad he couldn't secure mine," I half say, amused and annoyed.

The bounty hunter takes a deep breath. Not an expressive man, usually. Hardly ever does this man smile. It makes me sad thinking of what could have turned a man like him into a stone-cold killer. Most all his bounties come in, draped over the back of his horse. I can't even feel sorry for those souls. They broke the law, and the bounty hunter tracks them down to bring them to justice. It just so happens they're wanted dead or alive.

There's a tick on his jaw.

"He get under your skin, too?" I ask, leaning into him as Jed Warner steps out into the dining room and announces dinner is a big spread against the wall for us tonight.

I know for a fact, too, that Jed Warner's pockets aren't deep. So either he's not doing this out of the goodness of his heart, or someone else is footing the bill. My bet is on Davenport. He and Mr. Conway are after my half of the land to tunnel their railway through the mountain. My land happens to be the best route to lay the track leading into Deadwood.

The entire town sits inside a gulch at the base of the mountain.

"We'll talk about it later."

"Now?" I pull my hand from his arm.

"Oh, how cute! You two make the most adorable couple."

I suck in my breath and turn on my heel. My closest and dearest friend, Ella Mae, grins from ear to ear. Her new husband, Lincoln, stands at her side. His boots are worn, and his eyes are weary. But never mind Lincoln. I embrace Ella Mae, happy to see she's still in one piece. I whisper in her ear. "Does your father know you're back in town?"

The bounty hunter extends his hand to Lincoln. "I see you're still alive."

Considering Ella Mae marched the man in front of the judge with my shotgun, Shorty, at his back, he looks well for a married man. The judge pronounced them man and wife the same day as the bounty hunter and me.

"We've been staying here at the hotel for the past few days," she lowers her voice. "My father doesn't know we're here."

"I'd like to keep it that way," Lincoln adds.

"Still afraid to stand before the preacher?" I tease, and Lincoln pales. I guess marrying the preacher's daughter can make a man feel ill. Especially when Ella Mae disappeared and hasn't told her parents the good news yet.

"Dimples," the bounty hunter warns.

"Lincoln hasn't told his father, either" Ella Mae crosses her arms and glances over at her husband.

"It's my mother I worry about," Lincoln says, taking his cowboy hat off his head and twisting it in his hands. "She hasn't been in good health. I don't want to shock her with the news."

Ella Mae slaps him on the arm. "Your mother is as sturdy as an ox. You're afraid your mother won't like me, admit it?"

"Maybe we should step outside and discuss this?" Lincoln lowers his chin, his eyes locking on Ella Mae. Her cheeks turn a bright shade of pink, and she licks her lips. I'd say they've been doing a *whole* lot of discussing in private lately.

But how would I know? Since the bounty hunter and I got hitched two days ago, this is the first I've seen him.

"Still in the honeymoon phase." The gambler comes up behind me and clasps Lincoln on the shoulder. "Congratulations again on your wedding."

Ella Mae glows with the praise. I don't think I've ever seen a more beautiful bride.

"You go yourself a handsome one," Daphne's eyes sparkle.

Ella Mae retakes hold of Lincoln. "I'm the luckiest girl alive."

"Some of us are luckier than others," the gambler says. "You just need to know how to gather the right cards in your hand." And he looks straight at me.

"How's that working for you?" the bounty hunter asks.

The gambler pulls back his shoulders. "You might think you've won this hand, but the cards haven't all been dealt."

"Perhaps we should make plates for ourselves. All the hard work Mr. Warner put into hosting this meal, and we're letting it go cold," Daphne suggests.

I snuggle closer to the bounty hunter, feel him stiffen, and try to smile. Ella Mae gives me a curious look. She smiles wanly as she and Lincoln move toward the food.

I can feel the bounty hunter holding his breath. The muscles in his arm go taunt. Finally, I release him and watch as he excuses himself to join the others.

I want to reach out and grab him from leaving me alone. Maybe it's because he thinks I'm safe from the gambler making advances now that we're married.

It doesn't settle things in my gut, as those alluring green eyes still have a way of holding me hostage.

The gambler tugs on his lapels, those dimples of his form as he grins. "Trouble in paradise already, darlin'?"

"I don't believe that's any of your business."

"We're partners, darlin'. Remember, I own half of that claim. Whether or not you like it, you're my business."

"My marriage is not."

The bounty hunter holds a plate waiting for me to join him. He lifts a brow.

"If it's not working out, we can always go back to the judge, explain this misunderstanding, and clear up all this nonsense. You and I will be married. I'll even overlook your little indiscretion with Townes."

"There's no misunderstanding."

The gambler sets those emerald eyes on me again, cutting in deep. "Don't say I didn't give you a chance."

"I'm a married woman. There's nothing you can do to change that." I walk over and join the bounty hunter. He holds the plates as I pile on the feast. There are slices of ham and thick mashed potatoes. I pour on the gravy as the gambler ambles up beside me. I try to pay him no mind. On the other side of him, Lloyd Coose speaks with Daphne in line. I guess she wasn't quick enough to fall in line beside Weston.

Silverware clicks from the tables. Ruby and half the town have come out for tonight's gathering. I'm surprised Ella Mae's parents haven't shown up. Lincoln and Ella Mae come cozying up beside us. "Want to go first? You got married before us," Ella Mae says.

"You go on," I say, "We'll follow you."

Then I notice the bounty hunter's eyes. The usual stone-cold grey is blocked out by expanding pupils and a hooded look that sends alarms going off in my head.

Ella Mae rises on her tiptoes as Lincoln turns his head and plants one on her lips. My eyes widen. Oh. Oh my. I glance up at the bounty hunter. He's as still as a statue.

I don't touch him. I turn my back to the others and look him in the eyes. As much as it pains me, I say softly, "It's alright. I don't expect you to."

"Go on, kiss the man," Ella Mae declares once her lips are free again. I can feel everyone in the room staring at my back. I left my hair down this evening, not bothering with it in the rain. Even my hat hangs beside the bounty hunter's since I didn't want to draw much more attention to myself than I do wearing my cowboy boots.

I turn to Ella Mae. "We like to keep it private."

"Private?" Lincoln says, "You're married."

"In name only," I try to keep my voice down. Clacking silverware resumes. I can hear my heart beating.

"What do you mean it's in name only?" Ella Mae says it so loud that the gambler's eyes light up. "Is that so?"

And before I can say another word, the bounty hunter shoves me ahead. I move away to the table where Ella Mae and Lincoln follow. They sit across from us, but as I try to take my seat, the bounty hunter grabs me by the arm. He whirls me around, and his lips come crashing down on mine.

My heart nearly explodes in my chest, and as I lean into those earth-shattering lips, a slap echoes through the room. Immediately, the bounty hunter releases me, and I fall against the table. Ruby grabs my elbow and keeps me upright.

Over by the smorgasbord, Daphne screams at Lloyd Coose. "How dare you!"

Mr. Davenport rushes to her aside, and even Sheriff Bentely stands at the theatrics. The bounty hunter takes fewer strides to reach her, and Lloyd Coose shrugs. "You asked for it."

Daphne's eyes grow wide. "Arrest this man!" she says to the sheriff.

"For what? Kissing isn't no crime," Lloyd says. "You're a tease."

"You'll step away from Miss Davenport," Mr. Conway steps around him, keeping Daphne shielded. The bounty hunter puts his hand on his gun, and the sheriff is beside him.

"She's been flirting with me ever since I got here."

"I did no such thing," she draws back her shoulders. "You mistake my politeness, Sir."

"I believe you overstepped your bounds, Mr. Coose. You can return to the crew tonight," Mr. Conway stated.

"In this weather?" Coose laughed. "I think I'll be staying right here in the room I've got."

"Then by morning," Mr. Conway held out his hand. "I'll see you out."

Conway tossed down his plate, flood splattering to the floor. He leans in, hissing at Conway. "You think you're such a big man, but I know the truth. You want me to leave? Fine, I'll go. You can find another man to do your dirty work. I'm done."

He marches out of the room, Conway following him. Sheriff Bentely relaxes and turns to everyone. "It's over, folks. Let's get back to our meal."

As the bounty hunter approaches, he asks, "You okay?"

I swallow the words, begging to spill, nodding.

He pulls out my chair, and I sit. Around us, whispers and conversations resume. Daphne sits with her father, and the gambler sits between her and me. Across from her sits Warner and Lincoln, and Ella Mae.

"So, in name only?" The gambler picks up his glass and swirls the dark liquid. "Don't you worry, darlin', when I kiss you, it won't be for show."

I glance over at the bounty hunter. He's scowling and forking up a heap of mashed potatoes.

Something tells me it's going to be a long evening, and it's far from over.

2

There is a piano in the corner of the dining room. The keys sound rusty, but the gambler has no trouble striking up a tune and attracting the attention of most of the ladies. Hannah Baker and Lottie Larson stand near the piano. Hannah's never been married, and Lottie, who knows, they're the town's two most eligible ladies and biggest gossips.

Mr. Davenport stands by the fireplace with the sheriff, a few other gentlemen, and Mr. Harris.

Some tables are missing, and folks are waltzing to the gambler's tune. Amaryllis and Buck Dawson are the first to dance. Soon others follow, and Lincoln and Ella Mae sway in the center. It's romantic seeing them finally together. Ella Mae's gotten everything she's ever wanted. She glows with the joy radiating from inside her.

"What do you say, Dimples?" Is the bounty hunter really asking me to dance?

I shake my head.

"You don't want the gambler to think this is a fake marriage, do you?"

I crane my neck, thoughtful for a moment. A splash of hurt

runs down me. Is that why the bounty hunter kissed me and now wants to dance?

"No, thank you," I say.

I'm surprised Daphne isn't in the trio around the gambler. I bet my last dollar she knows how to dance.

And while I'm thinking about it, I glance around.

"What's the matter?" Ever since the bounty hunter kissed me, my belly does this funny little flip when he comes near me. I could hardly eat a bite, especially with the gambler and him crowding against me.

"Have you seen Daphne? I mean Miss Davenport."

"No." The bounty hunter narrows his gaze. "Mr. Conway seems to have disappeared too."

Interesting.

"I haven't seen either of them since they started serving the cake." Now that I think about it could have been before the cake.

I spy the sheriff heading in Ruby's direction; she's wearing a lovely red frock the shade of her name. Some ladies step aside, and I watch her step onto the dance floor with the sheriff.

I look over at the bounty hunter, and I know he's assessing every person in this room.

As the gambler ends his tune, Mr. Clark, a man hired by the railroad and staying at Ruby's place, takes the bench. Miles Clark is about my age, with an accent that makes a girl hang on his every word. He slips off his jacket, and he, too, shows off his musical talent.

The gambler has his sight set on one woman in this room. He walks straight past Hannah and Lottie through the dancers, and I clutch my skirt. My stomach drops as I see those eyes gleaming in my direction. He steps in front of me with his hand held out. "Jolene--."

Reverend Carter comes storming inside the dining room. Water rolls down from his hat and his coat. Behind him, Pearl, his wife, appears like a drown cat. Her hair sticks plastered to her face.

The air in the room grows cold. The dancers stop as quickly as the music dies. It doesn't take long for Reverend Carter to spot Ella Mae. He goes strutting right through the dance couples. Lincoln drops his hands from Ella Mae, puffs out his chest, and gives the good Reverend a nod. "Reverend Carter."

"Don't you, Reverend Carter me." He shakes his finger at Lincoln. "And you!" He points directly at Ella Mae. "Shame on you both!"

Pearl stays behind her husband, tugging on his hand. "Let's not make a spectacle, shall we? Perhaps we can talk about this at home."

"I'm not going home." Ella Mae tilts up her chin. She clasps Lincoln around the arm. "Lincoln's my husband, and I go where he goes."

"You'll march straight home, young lady," Reverend Carter shouts.

"No, father."

"Ella Mae, I think you should do as your father says." Lincoln tugs at his shirt collar.

Ella Mae's jaw drops, her eyes widen, then a look of fury comes over her.

"What kind of man doesn't ask for a girl's hand in marriage first before taking off with her?" Reverend Carter shoves his finger in Lincoln's chest.

While Lincoln steps back, Ella Mae holds her ground. "You have no authority over me anymore. Lincoln and I were married by the judge. If you don't believe me, ask Mr. Townes and Jo. They were our witnesses."

Reverend Carter swings his gaze to me, followed by Pearl.

"She's right." There is no forgiveness for lying to a preacher.

"And so did Jo and Mr. Townes. And if you don't mind, we're celebrating."

I pressed my hand to my heart. I don't think I've ever heard Ella Mae outright be disrespectful to her father.

"Ella Mae Carter," her mother exclaims.

"That's Mrs. Dawson to you."

Pearl's face scrunches up. Tears waver in those eyes. "I told you this would happen. Now another one of my girls has gone and run off with a man."

Ella Mae's posture wavers. She rushes to her mother. I can't hear what she says, but they're both crying.

Poor Lincoln looks like he swallowed a frog, and the Reverend looks mad enough to commit a felony. He yanks Pearl away. "She's not a daughter of ours. Not. Anymore."

Ella Mae's face falls. Her bottom lip trembles. She looks around at Lincoln's face, then back at her mother.

Bunching her skirt up in her hands, she takes off through the dining room.

Lincoln's face hardens as Buck Dawson and Amaryllis head his way.

"I guess the honeymoon is over," I say.

The bounty hunter remains at my side. The sheriff motions for Mr. Clark to play again.

"I should go check on Ella Mae." I don't give the bounty hunter a chance to react. I head for the doorway, stepping out into the foyer. Sherman eyes me warily from behind the reception counter. It wasn't too long ago I landed the man on his back when he was trying to return my clothes. Completely innocent and proper. I'd taken a bath over at the Swanson's sisters and changed into something cleaner and fancier. I dropped my pants off for Sherman to hold while I had dinner with the gambler.

Now I am married to the bounty hunter.

I guess the Swanson sisters didn't receive an invitation, or they didn't want to mess up their hair coming in the rain.

"Do you see Ella Mae go by?"

Sherman nods.

"Can you tell me which room? I want to check on her."

He tightens his lips. I move closer, crossing my arms. "Don't make me have to twist your arm."

"You're not the law. I'm not supposed to tell you. Privacy," he says.

"My best friend is upset. I need to check on her. Tell me what room our I'll go knocking on all of them. And that's after I twist your arm."

"Third floor, room 31." Sherman shrinks back, and I thank him before heading for the stairs. The fancy stairs curve up to the next floor. I have to walk down the red-carpeted hall to the next flight of stairs. It's a good thing these cowgirl boots are made for walking, not like those fancy heeled shoes Grace displays in her shop.

I spot Ella Mae and shout for her to wait so I can catch up to her, but she's not slowing down.

I'm halfway down the hall when I hear voices. As I draw near, Daphne steps out of the room. Her eyes go wide like a deer caught in the moment before a hunter releases his arrow. I almost stumble as she rushes past me, with her fan covering her face.

Suddenly, Ella Mae stops. She stares inside the opening of a room Daphne left. Ella Mae screams and screams. I rush, putting my arms around her.

Crumpled on the floor, Lloyd Coose lies with Mr. Conway standing over him inside the room.

I slap my hand over Ella Mae's mouth. It's the only way to muffle her screams. She slumps against me, her eyes still wide, and whimpers escaping through my fingers' hold.

Mr. Conway holds a gun in his hand. I back us away. Slowly. Mr. Conway holds up his hands as he rises. "It's not what it looks like, I swear."

"I believe you. Please. Let us pass." I slip my fingers off Ella Mae's mouth. She bolts down the hall into Lincoln's arms. He embraces her, his hand on the back of her head and around her waist. Around him, the sheriff, the bounty hunter, and several other men come charging forward.

The bounty hunter slips past me first. "He's dead."

The sheriff grabs the gun from Mr. Conway, pointing his own at the railroad owner. "You're under arrest."

"I didn't do it."

"Jo, you see him, do it?"

I shake my head, watching as Mr. Conway struggles and the sheriff cuffs him.

"No witness?"

"When Ella Mae and I came across him, Mr. Conway was hunched down beside Mr. Coose with a gun in his hand."

"Anything else, Dimples?"

"Daphne Davenport ran down the hall away from us."

"No shot?"

"Didn't hear it."

"None of us did, not with the music and the party," the sheriff mutters. "Come along, Mr. Conway. It's a good thing Judge Stevens is still in town."

Mr. Conway's eyes widen. "You have to believe me, sheriff. I didn't do this. I found him this way. I swear. The door was open, and the gun was lying beside him."

"And you picked it up?" The sheriff sighs. "Save your testimony for the judge."

There's something about the way Mr. Conway looks at me. His pleading eyes tug at a girl's sense of justice. "He'll get a trail, right?"

"Someone want to fetch the undertaker?" The sheriff holds

a gun to Mr. Conway's back, and the crowd parts. "I'll send my deputy over to question everyone. Nobody leave the hotel."

The bounty hunter stands in the doorway. "Lincoln, why don't you take your bride to your room? The rest of you with rooms, go to them and stay in them. Those without, return to the dining room and stay there."

"What's going on here?" Jed Warner pushes through the crowded hallway.

Ella Mae buries her face in Lincoln's shoulder as he leads her to the stairs going to the next floor. He keeps his hand on Ella Mae's head so she can't turn and see the dead body as they pass.

Blood seeps into the rug.

"There's been a murder. No one is to leave until the sheriff returns to question them."

"But he arrested the other man," someone shouts.

"A man has a right to claim innocent until proven guilty," the bounty hunter says, a shadow coming over his face. I have a feeling he knows more about that than anyone.

I go to reach for him, then remember the last time when he got all tense. I keep my hands to myself. Then he addresses me. "You should find Ruby and stay with her."

"Does this mean I can't leave town?" I ask.

"' Fraid so."

After my father was found shot behind the saloon a few weeks ago, the sheriff decided I couldn't leave town until the dispute over our claim was resolved.

Already, I've been gone from our claim for too long. Tail Feathers and his people might have been appeased by the tobacco and fire water I sent them to pay my father's debt, but with the railroad coming to town and their crew laying track in this direction, I have bigger worries.

Jed Warner steps around me and reaches for the door. "Must we display this for everyone to see? Where is Harrison?"

"If he's smart, he's staying somewhere dry," the bounty hunter says.

"If he's smart, he'll get this body out of my hotel." Warner pulls a handkerchief from his back pocket and covers his mouth.

"A man is dead." My head still reels with the thought.

"I'm going to lose customers. I've heard some of them asking downstairs if the boarding house has room," Warner rants.

"Can you blame them?" I hug myself, still rattled. Poor Ella Mae. At least she's got Lincoln to console her.

Warner cups the back of his neck. "I can't afford to lose business. If not for the rain, I think they'd have all rushed out of here."

"The sheriff told them to stay. He's got questions, and he'll be back shortly." The bounty hunter nods as Sherman stands at the end of the hall. His hand up and Adam's apple bobbing. "Mr. Warner?"

"What is it?" Warner shouts.

"Some of the guests are upset and want to leave."

"You should get down there. Your staff will need help, and they'll need your reassurance that everything is fine."

"Jo," the bounty hunter takes me by the shoulders. "Why don't you go with Warner? Find Ruby and head back to the boarding house."

I know a dismissal when I hear one.

3

"Why if it isn't Mrs. Chord Townes?"

I no more than step onto the boardwalk to escape the drizzling rain when I'm confronted. "If it isn't the woman who claims to be my mother."

"You've grown."

Had she stuck around while I was growing up, she'd know that I'm like a grizzly first thing in the morning, and not even the blackest coffee or sweetest rolls can soothe me. But, of course, seeing Polly Dean with her hair down and her black dress gone doesn't help either. She didn't mourn my father for long, if she mourned him at all.

"You think?" I keep walking.

Polly picks up her pace to keep in step with me. "Oh, I get it. You're mad at me."

Mad? No, I'm not mad. I'm hurt. I'm angry. I have very few memories of my mother. I hoped the bounty hunter, and I would be gone from this town before I had to be in the same company as this woman again, but God only knows why He keeps preventing me from returning to my home in the mountains.

If the gambler gets his way, I won't have a home any longer. But it's not me I'm worried about. It's Chitto and Tail Feathers and his people. With the railroad coming, the last thing I need is Tail Feathers getting out the war paint on those rail workers should they trespass on Standing Rock.

I grit my teeth and ask, "What do you want?"

"Is that any way to talk to your Momma?" Polly pouts. She's got her lips painted a deep shade of red and those eyes, the mirror of my own, trying to hook me with sympathy.

"You gave up being my mother when you left me with Earl up on that mountain."

"You make it sound as if I had a choice." She pants a little as we pass the cafe. I smell the freshly baked pie, making me think of the bounty hunter. Apple is my favorite.

"Will you slow down?" she tries to grab my arm, and I pull it away.

"I want to talk to you."

"You've had over twenty years," I tell her. "I have got business I need to attend, and it isn't with you." A pang of longing spreads inside me, the kind of a little girl who cried many a night for her momma. The one who watched the mothers in Chitto's tribe tend to their daughters, hug them, and teach them necessary skills. I learned while I watched. Earl taught me to make coffee, to pan for gold and silver. Ella Mae's mother taught me to sew, and when I got older, Earl dropped me at Ruby's to stay out of trouble, and she taught me a thing or two about cooking.

Now I'm looking at this woman. The one I wished all my life would come back, and it'd be like she never left.

I stop in front of the saloon. A chill crawls across my flesh. It's dark inside. I can't take my eyes off that door. Polly steps around, putting herself directly in my sights. "Jolene, darling." She sounds like the gambler. Putting her hands on my shoulders, she graces me with a smile. "All I'm asking is for you to give me a chance. I'm back now. Your father's gone, and he can't keep us apart any longer."

Pulling back my shoulders, I tilt my head. My heart tugs in one direction while my head pulls in common sense. "I don't have time for this."

"Why not?" Her eyes flash while her smile falters.

"None of your business."

"You are my business," she declares.

"Me or Earl's share of the land?"

Her lips part slightly. After all these years, she had enough nerve to show up in front of the judge in her black dress and want a piece of the Earl's claim. I can see why my father always kept her photo in the bottom of his boot. But, at this moment, I understand why he'd want to step on her a time or two.

Inside, the child in me slinks back to make room for the woman. For a moment, a ray of hope lightens my heart. But then Polly says, "If it wasn't for me, he wouldn't have that claim."

I pull my hat down low to shield my eyes and step onto the street. On the other side, the gambler stands in front of the bank. He tips his hat and reaches past me. Polly steps up on the boardwalk, her shawl draped overhead to protect her from the rain. "Why, there is a gentleman for you."

Polly keeps hold of the gambler's hand. She lets her shawl fall back down around her shoulders. "Polly Dean. Jolene's mother."

I try not to roll my eyes or gag.

"Pierce Weston," the gambler releases her hand, his hair glinting red where the strands are damp from the weather. He grins, showing off his dimples.

"You're the man who won my daughter's hand in marriage in a card game?" She clutches or shawl together. "Or was it the other man? I can't remember which one of you the judge married to my little girl."

Heading for the door, the gambler beats me to it. He holds it open. "I might not be Jolene's husband now, but I will." He winks at me while talking to Polly.

"I like a man who knows what he wants and doesn't give up." Polly places her hand on his arm. How dare she lay a hand on him in such a familiar manner?

"I take it I have your consent," the gambler asks.

Polly bats her lashes. "Of course, you do, and anything else you might think to call upon me in need."

Turning on my heel, I enter the bank before I barf. Polly follows behind.

"I've got business here," I say.

"You're not the only one." She sashays up to the teller line.

Campbell Reed sits behind a polished cherry desk. His dark sideburns run almost the entire way down the side of his face. He sits back in his upholstered chair, his hands clasped together. Silence fills the office as we wait.

The pine on the walls shines from a recent polish. As I sit there, the scents of tobacco and paper money filter through the air.

To my right, the gambler stands, arms crossed and chin tilted. To my left, the bounty hunter rests his hand on the butt of his six-shooter. I've discovered it's a habit for the bounty hunter. He pulls back his long leather jacket enough to reveal his gun belt and the six-shooter he carries against his leg. His near presences send tingles under my skin. Nothing in this world can wipe the memory of when his lips landed on mine. No matter his reasons, the memory has branded into my mind.

After last night's shenanigans, Ruby helped me out of my

green dress. At least I'll be able to breathe easier as Mr. Reed gives me the bad news.

Soon a man comes through the door, joining Jones, the claims clerk, standing off to the side. The gambler holds on to his lapels.

Someone clears their throat behind us.

"Judge Stevens had to move on to Silver Valley. Mr. Osterioh here has got everything in writing," Mr. Reed says. "Lavern, would you like to go over the details?"

Lavern Osterioh steps beside the desk, leaving Jones alone to witness this meeting. "Thank you, Mr. Reed." Lavern walks with a slight limp, dragging his left foot against the wood floor.

Clearing his throat, Lavern says, "After gathering the needed information, I've consulted with the claims office for the value of the land and, in accordance with Judge Steven's decision, have come up with a valuation of the claim."

The gambler waves his hand. "On with it."

Lavern gives the gambler a moment's attention, then turns it on me. "Miss Dean."

"Mrs. Townes," Reed corrects.

"Pardon." Lavern clears his threat a little more and says, "Mrs. Townes. It is my understanding that you own half of Dean's claim. It appears the railroad has made a sizeable offer to purchase the claim from the government."

"They can't do that!"

The bounty hunter puts his hand in front of me to keep me back. "Let him finish."

"Yes. Finish. I'm with Jolene. What does that mean? Purchase from the government?" the gambler asks. His posture goes ridged. His fancy suit doesn't appear as pressed as usual.

"The railroad can purchase the claim if it's unattended or the claim owner cannot pay and report the minerals mined." Lavern holds up the papers in his hands like we can read them. "It would revert back to government property."

"Which it's neither." I cross my arms.

"If you are here, and Mr. Weston is here, who is attending the claim?" Reed asks.

I give him the stink eye.

The bounty hunter puts his hand on my arm. It sends warmth to my heart. "A claim was filed a few weeks ago. There's no violation."

"Who is tending to the claim?" Reed asks.

I'm about to open my mouth and tell him it's none of his business when the bounty hunter says, "It's being watched as per the Sheriff's instructions while Jo is detained here in town for legal business."

"A claim has to be abandoned for more than a few weeks to revert," Jones adds.

The gambler nods his head.

Lavern clears his throat. "You are aware you have thirty days to purchase the other half of the land from Mr. Weston. If you don't, the land has been petitioned to sell to the railroad, and the government will claim the sell."

"Now, wait a minute!"

"Hold on right there!"

The gambler and I shout at the same time.

"The judge never mentioned anything about that." Leaping forward, the bounty hunter holds me back.

"Something smells rotten, darlin'." The gambler narrows his gaze on Mr. Reed.

The bank owner shrugs. "It's no matter to me."

"Why are we here and not in the lawyer's office?" The gambler questions, and I agree.

"I believe you need to let Mr. Osterioh finish," Reed says.

"This doesn't smell rotten. It smells like a wet rat caught in the rafters," I say. "The government's got no say about my land. It hasn't been abandoned, and I'm not about to let the government, the railroad, or anyone else get their hands on it."

M gaze lands on the gambler. Those emerald eyes of his don't sparkle as usual.

"Judge Stevens should be able to clear this all up," the bounty hunter says.

"You're welcome to talk to Judge Stevens when he returns to town," Lavern offers.

"When will that be?" the bounty hunter asks.

Lavern scratches his head. "Oh, I'd say next month sometime."

"Yeah, we'll wait," the gambler agrees.

"Remember, you have thirty days," Lavern says, clearing his throat again.

"You mean thirty-two," I correct him.

"Thirty?" Reed asks, appearing to enjoy this interaction.

"Actually, it's twenty-nine." Lavern points to the papers in this hand. "It's been three days since you saw the judge."

"But you still haven't told us how much I need to purchase the land," I almost shout at him. The bounty hunter holds me tight and gives my arm another squeeze.

Beside me, the gambler grins, dimples and all. Oh, how I want to smack it off his face. Every day less I have, the better the odds for him to keep his share.

"Mr. Jones?" Lavern addresses the claims clerk.

Jones adjusts his wire glasses. "Due to the railroad coming in and land values going up in certain areas, mind you." He peers at us from the sides of his eyes. "I figure the land is worth around five thousand dollars."

My heart nearly stops. "Thousand?"

Jones nods.

Those dimples on the gambler go even deeper.

"But that's for the whole thing?" the bounty hunter asks.

"Half," Jones takes a step back.

My heart plummets into my gut. "Half?" I squeak. "You're out of your mind."

I can't breathe. I clutch my chest. The bounty hunter never keeps his arm around me.

"I'd like to see the land assessment. Who was the surveyor?"

Lavern clears his throat and thrusts out the paper to the bounty hunter. The gambler goes silent, and it unnerves me. Those emerald eyes of his glint with reflections of gold.

"Since the railroad was already in the area, we used their surveyor," Reed supplies.

The bounty hunter snatches the paper, his fist turning a little white and the paper crumbling on the sides. "Coose. Lloyd Coose."

"The dead man?" I croak, my chest aching. "I thought he was a scout for the railroad."

"So did I," the bounty hunter says.

"It makes sense," the gambler adds his two cents. "The man goes out and scouts the area. He surveys it, reports to the railroad, and determines the cost and purchases the land."

"Is that right?" I look at the bounty hunter. "Seems on the high side for a purchase offer."

"The railroad would want to get the land for a bargain, not pay prime."

"Not necessarily," the bounty hunter looks at the paper again. "They don't always have to own the land. The government could hold the land, and they have the right of way to put their tracks through."

The gambler's jaw clenches. He peers at Reed the Lavern.

"We can have the land reassessed if you like," Reed offers. "But I must warn you, the market price could go up."

Up? "What's your deal in this?" I ask, feeling peeved.

"Nothing," Reed stands. "I understand where you are coming from, Mrs. Townes. I'm glad to offer as much assistance as I can. As a representative of the Deadwood Bank, I've been appointed to hold any monies you wish to deposit toward the purchase of the land in trust until you come up with the full amount or return it once the date has expired. You should also know, should you gain any money off the land, I will also hold it in trust until the land ownership is settled."

This isn't happening. "My father staked that claim fair and square, and you know it."

When Polly ran out on him, he added my name to the claim. He said he didn't want Polly to show up later, trying to steal all his hard work from under him.

Then he went and gambled it all away.

And the government wants it too. Why? A sinking feeling plummets in my stomach. Tail Feathers, Chitto, and the tribe. Could they possibly know?

"Easy, Jo," the bounty hunter hands back the paper to Lavern. My body trembles. He turns me to look into those stone-cold grey eyes. Then, as if he can read my thoughts, he says, "Not going to happen."

Lavern clears his throat again. He tucks the papers under his arm. "Let me know when you need the deed changed," he says more to Jones than any of us. Jones follows him out, avoiding looking at us.

When the door shuts again, I find the gambler with his hands in his pockets. "What are you so amused about?"

"Isn't a man allowed to be happy when he's about to hit the jackpot?" He leaves, whistling some riverboat tune as he goes.

"Not if the government takes hold of it," the bounty hunter smirks at the fall of the gambler's smile.

"What are we going to do?" If Lloyd Coose wasn't dead, I could kill him myself.

"Let's go see Sheriff Bentley," the bounty hunter says.

That's the best thing I've heard all day.

4

Inside the sheriff's office, a man with sandy blond hair and spurs on his boots sits at the desk. He's got his hat tipped over his face and a deputy star on his shirt.

The bounty hunter strides over and knocks the man's boots right off the desk. Startled, the man's hat tumbles down his chest as he scrambles to catch it, grab his gun and stop from falling over in his chair. The bounty hunter has quick reflexes when it comes to the draw. It takes my breath away seeing him in action.

"You'd best hand that over. Nice and easy," the deputy says.

"Is that right?" Slowly, the bounty hunter spins his gun and puts it back in the holster.

The deputy frowns, his hair skewed, and his gun still pointed at us.

"You'd best put that away before someone gets hurt," I say.

From inside a cell at the end of the room, Mr. Conway sits on a cot and snorts. "He'll pull his gun and shoot you dead before you pull back your hammer."

The deputy glances over at Mr. Conway. The bounty hunter reaches over, and, in a blink, the deputy is without a gun.

"Hey!" he exclaims. "You give that back."

The bounty hunter disarms the gun. "I think I'll keep a hold of this. We don't want anyone getting hurt. Where is Sheriff Bentely?"

"How do you know I'm not the sheriff?"

"You've got a deputy badge on, son," Mr. Conway states.

He's not wearing his fancy jacket, and his sleeves are rolled to his elbows. Mr. Conway sits with hands on his raised knees, the cot too low to the ground for his height.

It wasn't too long ago that I tried to lock myself in that cell to keep the gambler from marrying me. I glance over at the bounty hunter. He's still holding the gun, but he's not pointing it at anyone.

"I asked you a question," the bounty hunter says, his voice low and direct.

"He went to the cafe about an hour ago to grab breakfast," Mr. Conway stands up, pressing a hand to his back as he works out the kinks. I move toward him, and the deputy side-steps around the desk to get in my way.

"Whoa there," I hold up my hands. "I just wanted to talk to the man."

A tuff of hair falls over the deputy's forehead. "How do I know you and that fella haven't come to break him out?"

"If the sheriff feared someone coming to break me out, he wouldn't have left me with you," Mr. Conway states.

I press my lips together to keep from smiling.

"What's your name?" The bounty hunter asks.

"Lem Payne. *Deputy* Payne, and who are you?"

"Chord Townes."

Payne's face goes from curious to horrified in two-seconds flat. He points his finger at the bounty hunter, and I don't have the heart to tell him it's not nice to point at a man with a gun.

"I've heard of you," he says. "You're that ranger, aren't you?"

Sucking in a breath, I peer at the bounty hunter. His jaw has got that tick I've seen when he's upset. His eyes narrow, and my heart speeds up. I glance over at Payne. He's about to say something, and I interrupt. "Bounty hunter."

Mr. Conway plays with the side of his mustache. His eyes widen with curiosity.

"That's right. You're the outlaw killer."

I gulp as the bounty hunter's hand tightens around the gun. Any moment I fear he'll storm out or shoot someone. His past isn't a subject he likes to talk about. So, I try to change it for him, "And we're hunting a killer, which is why we need to talk to Mr. Conway and the sheriff, of course."

Deputy Payne glances between us. "Anything you came to discuss with the sheriff, you can say to me."

Chord flips the gun around and lays it on the desk, his hand still covering it. "How long ago did Sheriff Bentely swear you in?"

"Yesterday afternoon."

"Well, that explains it," I say.

"And you are?" Deputy Payne asks.

I hold out my hand. "Jo Dean."

"Townes," Mr. Conway corrects.

When Payne looks at the bounty hunter, he nods.

"But you said, Dean?"

I shrug. "We haven't been married long, still getting used to the name change."

"I haven't ever met a woman who was a bounty hunter."

"She's not," the bounty hunter says.

"I could be," I say.

He gives me a look that says, 'over my dead body,' and I lift a shoulder. I move over toward Mr. Conway. After all, I told Payne I wanted to talk to him.

"Lloyd Coose was more than a scout, wasn't he?"

"Why does his duties to the railroad concern you?" Mr. Conway asks.

I move closer to the bars. "How much did it cost you to alter the judge's decisions to steal my land?"

"Interesting."

"What?" I ask.

Behind me, the deputy sits back in his chair and takes back his gun. The bounty hunter lingers between us, his eyes on Payne and the gun.

"Put that away before you hurt someone, and I get blamed for another murder." Mr. Conway paces away from the bars. His eyes have dark rings from lack of sleep. Inside, his cell stinks of moldy straw and the chamber pot in the corner.

"How much did you pay?"

Mr. Conway sits back down in the cot. "I have no reason to bribe the law for favors, Mrs. Townes. Especially since your husband and I already reached an agreement."

Before the bounty hunter and I were hitched by the judge, I caught him in conversation with Mr. Conway and Mr. Davenport. Why that no-good son of a dog had gone behind my back! "Agreement?" I whirl around and slam into the bounty hunter's chest.

He looks over me at Mr. Conway. "Loose was a surveyor?"

Conway nodded. "I paid him and Harris to find the best route, acquire the land for the best prices."

"You mean cheapest?" I ask, glaring at the bounty hunter. "Except my land. No thanks to your scout. It now has a hefty price tag on it."

Conway leans back, tapping his chin. "You don't say."

It doesn't make sense to him either. Huh?

"Jo," the bounty hunter glances between Payne and Conway.

I pinch my lips, storing away this piece of knowledge for later. "What's this agreement you made concerning my land?"

"It won't matter," Mr. Conway says. "They send me to prison for murder. There won't be an agreement."

"Prison?" Deputy Payne makes a noise and slides his gun back into his holster. "They hang you for murder around here."

Mr. Conway's face goes white as a sheet. His eyes round out as large as saucers. "You have to help me."

"I'm sorry. Me and the bounty hunter only have twenty-nine days to secure my claim." And save Tail Feathers and his people from discovery.

Suddenly, I feel the weight of an entire population on my shoulders.

"Please," Conway pleads in a hoarse whisper. "I am innocent. You can't let them hang an innocent man."

The bounty hunter takes a good, long look at Conway. I see the edge of the hardness in his eyes soften. Before letting him say yes, I add, "It'll cost you."

"Jo," the bounty hunter says.

"No." I hold up my hand. "How else will I get the money to keep my claim? Either I have the money, or the government allows the railroad to have it." I place my hands on my hips. "I get to keep my land, and in return, we'll find the killer, that is, if you're innocent."

"I think you should let that up to the sheriff and his deputy," the bounty hunter says.

I glance over my shoulder at Deputy Payne. He's spinning his hat on a finger. Raising a brow at the bounty hunter, I say, "I don't need your help. I found my father's killer without you."

"I seem to remember you being drugged and would have died if I hadn't found and rescued you."

I wave my hand. "I am not about to make that mistake again."

"Whatever the cost, I'm willing to pay," Conway says.

"Five grand." I hold my hand through the bars.

Conway stands. He looks at the bounty hunter. "We have a deal."

He reaches beside me, shakes the bounty hunter's hand, and I withdraw mine, trying not to offend. Men and their narrow-minded views about dealing with women. I huff.

"And our other agreement?" the bounty hunter asks.

"I'll see that it's honored," Mr. Conway states. "If someone paid off the judge, I swear on my life, it isn't me."

For a man with time running out, I believe him. Who would want to pay off the judge and make sure the land went to the railroad? Lloyd Coose.

Which would make the gambler look like a suspect again, or worse — me.

The door to the sheriff's office opens, and Deputy Payne jumps to his feet. Surprised, Daphne Davenport stops short inside. Her bonnet dripping with rain, a basket hanging from her arm. "I brought Mr. Conway some provisions."

"Where is your father?" Mr. Conway asks.

She shakes her head. "He went to see a lawyer about getting you out of here."

The bounty hunter and I both look at each other.

The deputy takes the basket from Daphne and sits it on the desk as we leave.

Outside, the rain continues steadily as ever. I can't imagine that there will be much more left in those dark-rimmed clouds after this. We don't go far when I stop in front of the wanted posters outside the Sheriff's window. I see Daphne standing with her hand over Mr. Conway's.

The bounty hunter continues to walk away.

"Where are you going?"

He pulls his long duster around him as the wind shifts. "Café. You coming?"

"I want to know what agreement you have with Conway and Davenport, and don't tell me it's part of the secret of your past I can't ask. You might be my husband, in name only," I add, "but that's still my land, and there are still a lot of things at risk."

He glances over his shoulder. "Which is why we should discuss this over pie and coffee."

"I'm not hungry. I ate breakfast at Ruby's."

"You can't tell me you don't want pie, Dimples."

I both hate and love it when the bounty hunter uses the nickname he bestowed on me. While the gambler has dimples when he grins, I do too, and apparently, the bounty hunter likes them. A little tingle of delight burst in my belly, of course, for the mention of pie.

"Fine, but don't you go running out on me, bounty hunter."

He waits until I stride shoulder to shoulder with him and wraps his arm around me as I adjust my hat for the rain. The bounty hunter leans against me. The potentate, like the cigars he smokes, makes me relax.

Leaning his head closer, he says, "You know, I have a name. You can call me Chord."

"And you can call me Jo."

He smirks, "Anything you say, Dimples."

5

Who would have thought a girl like me could be seduced by something as simple as pie? Not any pie, mind you, but fresh from Thompson's bakery. Fresh scents of apple waft inside the tiny cafe, and on the other side, a door hangs open for all the heavenly scents to drift through.

Several folks sit at tables while the waitress fills their coffee cups. After the morning we've had, I deserve a slice of pie, a cup of good coffee, and to get to know my husband.

We made a deal.

I don't pry into his secrets from the past, and he keeps mine. If not for Tail Feathers and his tribe, I wouldn't have survived living away from humanity all these years. Chitto might have tried to claim me as his wife at one time, but without him, I would never have learned to snare a rabbit, where to forage for berries, and how to grow anything in the stiff soil or to catch a fish upstream. When my father, Earl, wasn't digging into the mountain, we'd built a canal to run water and sift through the dirt and rock to find gold and silver.

Quickly, I learned the treasures of our land were more than colored rocks. The true treasures lay within the people living in the mountains, trying to preserve their way of life and protect what was theirs first. If I don't protect them, who will?

The calvary, the railroad, none of them care about the people or family or whose was here first. All they see are dollar signs and land. It's what brought my father this far.

Ornery old goat. Thinking about him brings pain to my heart. God rest his soul. He brought this trouble on me.

The bounty hunter stands by a chair at a table, waiting. The closer I get. He pulls out the chair, about to take a seat.

Over by the wall, I hear a snort, then see the gambler rise from his breakfast. "Allow me, darlin', some men have no manners where a lady is concerned."

The gambler walks past the bounty hunter, takes my chair, and holds it out for me. The bounty hunter scowls. There's a challenge in the gambler's face. A little flutter ripples in my belly. I'm hungry, that's all. But the bounty hunter's scowl darkens as the gambler pushes in my chair. "You sure you want to sit with him? You can always join me? I don't mind sharing my table with your company or my meal."

His eyes sparkle. His hand lingers on the back of my chair. There's a whole different meaning in those eyes.

The bounty hunter waves to the waitress. "My wife and I would like two slices of pie and coffee."

The gambler smirks. "My offer is always open."

Watching him walk back to his table, I tilt my head. He's got a plate full of eggs and fried ham. He picks up his coffee, sipping as he returns my gaze.

"Dimples," the bounty hunter's voice rumbles as he calls me that nickname again. His eyes have hooded. Tingles shot up my spine. Then I realize the waitress is behind me with pie, and it's not me those eyes are lusting after. She places the pie on the table, a much larger slice for my bounty hunter, and promises to return with the coffee.

"You shouldn't encourage him."

Behind the bounty hunter, the gambler chomps on a piece of bacon and wiggles his brows at me. It makes me smile, and I know I shouldn't.

"See what I mean," he says.

The waitress comes, brings cups, and pours coffee. She's back in a flash with cream, just the way the bounty hunter likes it.

Cream is a luxury we never had living up in our shack against the mountain. Reverend Carter once preached that we should avoid temptations. They're addictive, and they can lead a man astray. I'm no man. Licking my lips, I reach for my coffee, but the bounty hunter is quicker. His hand covers the mug first, then over-top mine.

It's warm. His fingers against mine send prickles against my palm. Immediately, I jerk my hand away. He switches our mugs. "Try it."

"You all need anything else?" the waitress asks. She's looking at my bounty hunter. There's not a woman in Deadwood who isn't entranced by him.

He's mine.

Satisfaction dissipates when I spot the gambler still watching, still eating slowly, winking, grinning, and flirting from afar. The man has no shame.

"Another cup and some sugar."

"Is someone else joining us?" I ask.

"Nope." The bounty hunter slides his mug toward me. "You should try it."

"No, thank you."

"Never took you for one to be afraid of trying new things," he counters.

"We're not here for me to try different things in my coffee."

"Sure, we are." He jerks his chin toward the gambler behind us. Sighing, I pull the coffee cup from his grasp, our fingers brushing. My cheeks warm, and not because the gambler has his eyes on me again.

"We're not to have that talk, are we?"

"Drink your coffee, Dimples," he says, and I see the answer written in the blank expression on his face. The man is like a locked safe. There's no chance he's opening up about anything with the gambler close by.

"I'll drink mine, and you drink yours," I say.

"Nice try," he tugs at my plate, taking my pie away. I reach for it, but he is tougher and quicker than most. "Drink, or I eat your pie."

I've never been one to back down from a challenge. Sorry, Reverend Carter. I pick up the warm cup and bring it to my lips. Cringing. Certain I won't like it.

Wrong. The cream makes it taste smoother. It's not as strong as what I'm used to drinking. I take another sip, and the bounty hunter gives back my cup. "Now try this one."

The waitress brings an extra cup and a sugar container and puts them down between us. The bounty hunter slides it in my direction, pulling his close to his side of the table again.

I lick my lips, wanting more.

"Liked that one, didn't you?" He says it with amusement in his voice.

"Maybe."

Even the waitress stands close by, watching our exchange. Finally, the bounty hunter adds sugar to the third cup. "Drink."

I love it when he's demanding. Never thought a cowgirl like me would be the type to swoon over authority.

"Fine," I say, acting like it's some chore. Smelling it first, it's not changed its scent. Not like the cream. Taking a sip, I am unsure. After another, I shake my head. "Too sweet."

"And here I thought you had a sweet tooth," he says.

"I just love apples."

"Noted."

He asks the waitress for cream, and she takes away the cup with the sugar added. Sliding back my pie, he takes a long gulp of his coffee. My breath hitches in my throat as he swallows. A flash of our kiss at the hotel haunts me. Seeing his lips covering where mine had been moments ago making me flush.

His eyes hood, and this time he's not looking at pie. The waitress returns and pours some cream into my coffee. She's gone at the call of the gambler. The bounty hunter's expression hasn't changed. I duck my head and dig into my pie.

Maybe Reverend Carter was right after all. One taste isn't enough. I dare a glance at the bounty hunter. It's done right, sinful.

While I enjoy my coffee, the bounty hunter polishes off his pie. Slow to bite into my own, I choose my words wisely. One way or another, I'm going to find out what agreement the bounty hunter made with Conway and Davenport. Deciding to take the safer route of decision for now. "We should probably figure out our first move."

"You're going to have to stay with Ruby until I figure this out."

"You mean 'we' figure it out? I'm not letting you get the bounty alone."

"Don't trust me?" He looks at me that way, and I don't trust myself. So I play with my fork by stabbing a chunk of apple into my pie.

"I've got 29 days to secure my land. After that, it'll take too long for the judge to return. I can't afford not to cash in on our deal with Conway. We find the killer, and I get the money."

"Which is why I'll handle it," he finishes his coffee.

"I need that money."

"I know." The bounty hunter lets go of his cup, his fingers sliding toward my hand, but a second later, he curls them and pulls back.

"It will do no good getting yourself killed."

I stuff a chunk of pie in my mouth before I say something I'll regret later. Chewing, I give him a stern look. It doesn't phase him. I see we're not going to agree on this, so I keep going, determined to find the actual killer, if there is one, and get that bounty money from Conway.

"What about Daphne Davenport?"

"What about her?" He takes another bite.

"She was there with him at the scene of the crime."

I take a bite as he mulls it over. Warm apple fills my mouth, and I close my eyes, savoring the taste. When I open my eyes again, the bounty hunter leans back, his eyes hooded, watching me.

Licking my lips, I dig in for another bite while the bounty hunter drains his coffee. Those eyes are as dangerous as the gun he carries. The moment disappears as the waitress comes hurrying over to refill it. I try not to roll my eyes. She admires my bounty hunter as he adds cream and stirs.

"It's a possibility. Someone shot him with his own gun."

"How do you know?"

"Conway doesn't carry. Coose's gun belt was empty."

He's right. As I think back to the hotel that night, Lloyd Coose had a gun belt strapped around his waist. What did a surveyor need a gun belt for? As a scout, he probably had to defend himself. It's wild territory the further west you go.

"Conway still could have shot Coose."

"True." The bounty hunter says, "and so could anyone else."

"Pathetic."

We both look up, and the gambler pulls a chair close to our table and takes a seat.

"No one invited you," the bounty hunter points out, but it doesn't stop the gambler from joining us.

He brings along his coffee, putting on one of his debonair smiles to catch the waitress's attention.

"I couldn't help overhearing. It wouldn't do to have Mr. Conway in jail, guilty or not."

"Don't you have a card game to get to?" the bounty hunter asks.

The gambler straightens his jacket, leaning away as the waitress comes to fill his coffee again. She glances at his empty table and stack of empty dishes. "Don't forget to pay for that," she says.

"Don't you worry," the gambler says, "I'll see you get taken care of."

I roll my eyes. He's crafty. I'll give him credit. So crafty, while he thought we would get married, he tried to use my credit at the mercantile and accumulated debt with people in town believing we were hitched.

Weston might fool everyone around him, but he doesn't fool me. I know he's got money, but I also know gambling can take it away in a flash of an ace. I wonder if he's down and out again. His half of the land won't be worth anything if I don't pay up.

"Later. Since Glen Adams got sent to the Iron Bar Hotel, the saloon has been closed. However, Mr. Warner has been kind enough to offer rooms in the hotel for such endeavors in the meantime. Although, I'd say this is more pressing business, is it not?"

"It's not your business," the bounty hunter says.

"I figure it is," the gambler adds sugar to his coffee.

"How is that?" I take another bite of my pie.

The gambler's eyes land on my half-eaten pie, and I pull it closer to me. There are some things a cowgirl doesn't share. Her boots, her man, and the plate she's eating from.

"I have a stake in this, too, darlin'. We both lose if the government takes hold of our claim." He picks up his cup of steaming coffee. "And I intended to get my money, all of it." He looks at me.

Pie gets caught in my throat, and I choke. The gambler reaches over, but the bounty hunter is quicker to pound me on the back. Once I can swallow and breathe again, the bounty hunter pulls his chair closer to mine.

"You'll get what's coming to you," the bounty hunter says.

"Not enough. As I see it, I got cheated, and I don't like to get cheated." This time, his glare points toward the bounty hunter.

"Says the man who gambles for a living."

Hurriedly, I finish my pie. Even if it kills me, I'm not leaving a single bite go to waste. Any minute, I suspect the bounty hunter will grab me, and we'll go.

"At least I don't kill people for a living."

I toss my cloth napkin between them. "If you two don't mind, I have a killer to find." I go to stand when they both take hold of me by the arm simultaneously.

"You can't go after a killer on your own," says the bounty hunter.

"Then I suggest you come with me," I say to him.

"Not if I get to him first," the gambler says.

Who said it was asking? I know the first place I'm going hunting, and neither of the men can follow me there.

6

Rumor has it that Daphne Davenport is feeling under the weather. No one has seen her since the discovery of Coose's body. Her father and Mr. Gilbert haven't left the hotel. They've been conducting business in Warner's office. I know this because one of Ruby's boarders, Mr. Clark, was hired by the railroad as their station master here in Deadwood. Plans are to construct the new station as soon as the supplies arrive. It'll take months, if not years, to tunnel through the mountains.

Mr. Clark is a friendly man. We have tea, as he and Ruby prefer their brewed herbs. Another dreary afternoon goes by where the bounty hunter leaves me at the boarding house, trying to command me like a child to stay inside and out of trouble. Ruby's making fried potatoes and roasted chicken for supper. When I got up this morning, she'd chopped the head off a chicken. I found Sheriff Bentely with blood on his hands, Ruby with feathers in her hair and the smock over her dress.

I didn't take Mr. Clark for a man afraid of a bit of blood, but I offered to distract him from the gruesome deed of watching Ruby pluck the plump hen in preparation for throwing it in the pot for tonight.

Sheriff Bentely scooted out the back before I could talk to him, but I am grateful Mr. Clark is such a helpful man. He's another of those addictions, with his quirky voice for being raised across the ocean.

There's not much for him to do, helping with the telegraph office while waiting for the station to get built. Mr. Harris and Mr. Davenport were hoping the crew would come before the May Festival.

What better time to celebrate the railroad coming through than a time when the whole town gathers?

It makes me think of the green dress I've got stashed away up in my room. I don't plan on wearing it again until the May festival. Although, part of me plans to solve who murdered Coose, pay off my land, and return to my claim long before the celebration starts.

According to a piece of paper, the bounty hunter might be my husband, but I learned a long time ago not to rely on a man for anything. In the end, it will cause you heartbreak and trouble. I couldn't even trust my father. He gambled me away.

While everyone is off doing their afternoon chores, Mr. Clark heads to the telegraph office, and I sneak away to the hotel. The bounty hunter never tells me where he's going. Since this marriage deal of ours is all for show, I figure I'm not going to be one of those wives; you know, the kind who need to know where their men are at all times. In return, I figure I don't have to tell him either.

Hearing how Daphne is under the weather, I figure I should pay her a visit. Besides my best friend Ella Mae and Ruby, Daphne is the only other female in town I'll give the time of day.

It's a good thing I'm wearing my cowgirl boots and my hat, for the rain never lets up. These April showers are at least holding up the railroad from trying to push through the mountain. Tail Feathers and his tribe are probably hunkered down out of sight. So maybe this rain isn't so bad after all.

I tap the mud from my boots outside the hotel. Mr. Clark was kind enough to walk with me this far before I crossed the street. Inside, Sherman operates the desk. Damp from the rain, I shiver, walking into the hotel lobby. They've got fires blazing in the dining room to the right. Behind the desk, the wide stairs leading to everyone's rooms are to the left.

"Morning, Sherman," I take off my hat and let my unruly waves and curls fall down my back.

"Mrs. Townes," he says my name in reserve, eyeing me like I'm a rattler ready to strike. "The dining room is reserved for guests only."

"I haven't come to eat but thank you."

He plays with a pencil in his hand. He's got a few years on me, but Sherman's not a bad looking man. Any single woman in town would find him pleasing to the eye.

"What have you come for?" He taps his pencil on the desk.

"I've come to see Daphne Davenport. She's a friend of mine." Okay, maybe I'm pushing it a little about the friend part.

Sherman frowns. He's not wearing a jacket, and his shirt sleeves are too long. "You don't need to check in to visit a guest."

"Right, but I need to know what room she's in."

Sherman closes the guest registry book in front of him. Pulling back his shoulders, he says, "Guest room numbers are private."

"But you told me Ella Mae's."

He stares straight ahead. "A mistake I won't make again."

Guilt tugs at me. There won't be getting any information from him. "I'll just head on up to visit Ella Mae."

"You can't."

"What not?" I ask.

"She's not here."

"Oh." I wait, hoping he'll explain. He stares at me, closed-mouthed.

Sighing, I push back a few strands of my hair. "She and Lincoln have checked out. Did they say if they were headed to the ranch?"

Nope, he's not going to answer.

"Fine. I'll find Daphne on my own." I head for the stairs.

Sherman rushes around his desk and blocks the stairs. "You can't do that."

"And why not?" Hands on my hip, I level my gaze on him.

Above, the booming voice of Mr. Davenport talking with Mr. Warner comes down the stairs. Warner scowls at me, or maybe it's Sherman.

"Mrs. Townes," Mr. Davenport opens his arms wide, smiling. "How are you?"

"I'd be better if Mr. Warner's clerk would allow me to pass. I've come to check on Daphne. I heard she's feeling under the weather."

Warner is the first to reach the bottom of the stairs. With his hand, he motions for Sherman to scoot back. The hotel clerk returns to his desk, but not before giving me a stern glance of his own.

"I'm afraid recent events have taken a toll on her. Thomas's incarceration has the poor dear in bed." Mr. Davenport puts on a sad smile. "He's been a close family friend and business partner for many years."

"I'm so sorry. I was hoping to visit with her, maybe invite her for a cup of tea." Thanks to Ruby, I've been slowly adjusting to the taste. What is it with the women of this town and their afternoon teas? I always thought it was a thing of the east.

By the way, Mr. Davenport assesses me. I know I'm not wearing the right outfit. I've got one suitable dress, the green one, and I was trying to save it for special occasions.

"Daphne offered to help me with a few female things. Perhaps I can be of a distraction to her."

Warner looks skeptical but curious. I nod to him. Last week, he expressed his interest in Miss Davenport. Silently, I give him a look, telling him I'll put in a good word for him. His shoulders relax, and some of the tension in his face dissolves.

"I'll have one of my kitchen staff prepare tea and deliver it to Miss Davenport's room."

We both turn our attention to Mr. Davenport as he contemplates the proposal. He scratches his balding head. "Daphne has been missing some of her lady friends back home. I can see how her assistance would be of value to you." His eyes narrow, taking me in from head to toe. "I believe it would cheer Daphne up, and Mr. Townes needs a properly behaving wife."

"Indeed." Warner clasps his hands together. "Sherman, call for one of the kitchen staff to prepare a proper tea and deliver it to Miss Davenport's room. Make sure it's for two."

"Yes, Sir." Sherman grunts.

"I'll be happy to escort you to Miss Davenport's room," Warner offers.

"No need," Mr. Davenport interrupts. "We've business to finish. Daphne is in the suite on the first landing, room six."

"Thank you." I leave the men and head up the stairs.

"Mrs. Townes." Then he repeats it, and I realize he's talking to me. "Mrs. Townes."

"Yes?" I glance back.

"You and your husband should join us for dinner this evening."

Is he asking? What will the bounty hunter say if I speak for us? The last place I want to be is dining again in this stuffy hotel after the previous events. Thinking of the chicken dinner Ruby's preparing makes my mouth water, but the more time I spend in this hotel might lead me to clues to solve Cooses' murder. Mr. Davenport might know something. I'm sure he does.

So, I smile brightly and say, "Of course, it would be our pleasure."

Later, I'll worry about finding the bounty hunter and giving him the news.

Daphne's room is adorned in gold. The paper on the wall is a foil damask, and all the cherry wood furniture gleams. It took a few moments for her to open the door. Her eyes widen. I guess I'm the last person she expected to see.

"Jo-Dee," Her hand flies up to her heart. "Whatever do I owe this visit?"

She's got a hankie in her hand and long ruffled lace hanging down from her elbows. Her dress is a few shades darker than the gold on the walls. Her dark, almost black hair hangs loose down her back. It's not polite to ask a woman her age, but with her hair down, Miss Davenport appears half my age. And I wonder.

"I was concerned after last evening. You mind if I come in?"

Daphne chews on her lip, glancing either way down the hall.

"Your father thought it would be good for us to visit," I add. "Mr. Warner is sending up tea for us."

Her lips turn down at the mention of Warner. "Then you must come in. And when Mr. Warner delivers the tea, you must fetch it from him."

A square table sits by the window with two chairs. Each one has brown leather seats with brass tacks around the edges. Daphne takes a seat and sighs.

"I knew it was only a matter of time before you came to me," she says.

"I wanted to ask you some questions."

"Of course, you do," she laughs. "I feel bad for your husband."

Now I'm the one with the frown.

She waves her hand. "Sit. The very least I can do is help you with your dilemma. After all, you did me a favor not marrying Pierce."

Pierce as in Pierce Weston, my gambler? No. He's not mine. That's not what I meant. I take a seat. "I won't take up much of your time. I understand how distressed you must be after last night." It distressed Ella Mae, and it unsettled me, too.

I've seen plenty of dead things in the mountains. Seeing someone recently murdered still causes all the hairs on my arms to rise.

"It's going to take more time than you think." She tilts her head. "We've got a lot of work to do."

"Then you'll help me help Mr. Conway."

She squints at me. "Mr. Conway? Thomas?" Her hand returns to press against her heart. The golden dress she wears has a high collar, something I have seen the old matrons wear in town going to church. Daphne also has a cameo broach at the base of her throat.

She grimaces, changing the subject. "We need to get you back in a dress. I'm sure the bounty hunter can afford to buy you one."

"He did. It's the one I wore last night."

"I don't blame you for not putting it back on today." She

picks up the fan from the table and waves it in front of herself. Looking out the window, a wagon goes down the street, pulled by a team of horses and several riders around it. "I told Thomas to stay out of it. My father would have handled it."

"Did you know Lloyd Coose?"

She lowers the fan. "He drops in from time to time to report to my father or Thomas." She uses his name as if he were a family member. I try to think nothing of it, as she has done the same with the gambler, referring to him by his first name.

"I don't like the way the man looks at me." She shimmies her shoulders. "My father has threatened to marry me off."

"Because of Coose?"

Daphne shakes her head. "Because I'm of age, and men look at me. I'm a real beauty, you know. A rare gem like the ones men mine for, or at least Thomas has told me."

A knock comes on the door.

"Get that, won't you?" then she whispers, "Don't let Mr. Warner inside my room. The man forever tries to impose his presence on me."

She's not wrong. Warner stands on the other side at the door with a tray of tea and small sandwiches. "I'll take this in for you," Mr. Warner says. "It's heavy."

Daphne moves to the corner by her bed, where Warner can't see her.

"I can take it." I hold out my arms.

"I insist," Mr. Warner tries to press forward.

"Miss Davenport isn't in the proper attire for male company. You'll have to excuse us this afternoon, as she feels under the weather. We appreciate the tea, and if you give me the tray, I'll take care of it."

"I see." Warner pulls back his shoulders. His tie is perfect, and his hair is feathered near his ears.

"I'll let her know you inquired about her and brought the tea," I say, gently taking the tray.

He nods, his lips thinning.

After turning with the tray in my arms, I used my foot to close the door. Daphne's hands go over her mouth, and she giggles. As I sit the tray down on the table, she says, "You closed it right in his face."

Warner has too many manners to open a door even if it's not locked to come into a guest's room. As large as this one is, I'd say Daphne has gotten one of his best suites. There is an adjourning room to the left, and I wonder if it leads to her father's room or a washroom. I don't ask, but I suspect the latter.

Daphne comes back, sits, and stares at me.

I take a seat, but she makes no move to reach for her tea.

I reach for a sandwich, and she slaps my fingers. "Decorum, Jo-Dee."

Hands on her lap, her shoulders pulled back and her chin up, she gives me a lesson on how to properly serve and drink tea. "I noticed that when we had tea at the boarding house, your adequate was lacking. I'm not surprised you'd come to me. We'll have you acting like a lady in no time."

"I don't have to act like a lady to be a woman. God did that when I was born," I say.

Daphne ignores me. She pours the tea, adds two spoons of sugar to hers, and reaches for mine. I cover the cup. "No sugar."

She shrugs, and I allow her to fill mine with a bit of cream. "What happened to the traveling gown Mr. Weston purchased for you?"

I returned it to Grace. The gambler hadn't paid for it. He'd put it on credit, probably in my name, like most things he tried to run up credit on in my name when he almost had the whole town convinced I was his wife.

"It wasn't a good fit." Like all the other dresses. Pearl, Ella Mae's mother, had given me a yellow one. It was too short and showed my cowgirl boots. Amaryllis gave me one, daring to stay the least, but then it got ruined when I caught my father's killer.

Okay, maybe the bounty hunter helped me a little.

"My green one is fine." I sip my tea and try to get back to the real reason for my visit. "Did you see Mr. Conway shot Coose?"

Daphne pales. "Jo-Dee, it is impolite to bring up such manners. At least first thing. There are pleasantries."

"Do you want to talk about the weather?"

She pauses at my tone, then says, "I have already discussed it with the sheriff. I don't wish to talk about it anymore."

Putting down my tea and level with her. "If I don't find the killer, I can't get the bounty money I need to buy the half of my land, then *Pierce*," I say his name, "Is going to have my marriage annulled so he can marry me and gain the other half for himself."

I don't tell her about the government and the chance of losing my land since it's really none of her business.

Daphne's lips push out. It takes a moment, then the light goes off in those eyes in understanding. "He can't do that. He has to marry me."

Surely, she didn't want him anymore. There are way better options for husbands, but I can see by the spark in her lavender eyes that she's one of those stubborn types.

"Why do you want to marry the gambler?" I ask. "Why not Mr. Warner?"

Making a face, she sips her tea. Okay, maybe not warner. At least Warner owns a hotel and has the means to support a wife.

Daphne glances back out the window. Holding her cup,

warming her hands between sips, she says, "I told you Daddy wanted to marry me off. He has chosen someone, and the arrangements are made."

"You don't like who he picked."

She shakes her head.

"Have you told him?"

She snorts and almost spills her tea. Sitting it down, she gets to her feet. "Oh, Jo-Dee, you do not know what it is to become a woman, do you?"

I glance down at the sisters, then back up at her. "I think I know right well, thank you."

"Sometimes I envy you," she says. "Mind you, I don't know how a woman can survive out there in the wilderness without all the amenities of town. It's no wonder you are as you are."

I try not to take offense.

"You must be relieved having a bounty hunter for a husband. Father says we'll be staying here in Deadwood for a while until the tracks come through and they build the station. He and Mr. Harris have had no choice but to take drastic measures to ensure the project finishes. Daddy will lose a lot of money thanks to Thomas if it doesn't."

"I see," I don't, so I ask. "How did Coose fit in again?"

She sighs and sits back down. Her hands clasped on her lap. Her shoulders are back as she sits in perfect posture. "It's my fault. My father's, really. Which is why I'm so glad you didn't marry Pierce. When we're married, he'll take me out of this dreadful town, and we'll travel on the riverboat he talks about and live in a big house with lots of land and a housekeeper."

That doesn't sound dreamy at all, but I hear it in her voice. "Wouldn't you have gotten that with the man your father has set up for you?"

The dream fades in her eyes. She picks up a tiny sandwich.

"Not for a long time, I suppose. We'll probably end up living back in one of the railcars like we did getting here. The train doesn't end here. Thomas has the idea of running through the Black Hills and even to California."

Those are big ideas indeed.

"He thinks he is protecting me." She blinks and nibbles at her tiny sandwich.

"You mean he thinks you killed Coose? Did you?" I pick one up, amused by the small size, no bigger than two fingers together.

"Whatever would make you think a thing like that? Of course, I didn't!"

"You were running down the hall from his room, and you went to visit him at the jail."

Daphne takes a deep breath and says, "I was worried about him."

"You mean Mr. Conway?"

"Obviously, it wasn't the dead man." She huffs. "I had heard them arguing. I knew it had to be about me."

"Who was he arguing with?"

"Thomas." Her eyes well up with tears. "Then I saw him."

"You mean Coose and Thomas."

"Like I told the sheriff, I never heard the gun, but I saw him lying there, and then Thomas came in from behind, but I could have sworn I heard him from inside the room."

Interesting. I stuff the sandwich piece in my mouth, one bite, trying to act casual about asking someone if they are a murderer.

Her eyes go wide. "Jo-Dee! Like this," she says, taking a small bite to demonstrate. No wonder the bounty hunter hasn't asked me to dinner, and we always eat at Ruby's. Could it be he's ashamed of me?

The gambler took me to dinner once, and tonight we're having dinner with Mr. Davenport. Maybe I need to take a few lessons from Daphne. The more time I spend with her, the more she talks, and the more she talks, the more I can find out to help me catch a killer and cash in on the bounty I need to save my land.

"I see we have our work cut out for us," Daphne says.

7

Another stuffy dinner at the hotel. I'm not looking forward to it in the least. "And don't forget to wear a dress," echoes in my mind in Daphne's pitched voice. Why is it that a woman is always expected to wear a dress for these occasions?

Guilty rides inside me. Ruby's kitchen smells of roasting chicken. There is a house full of boarders this week thanks to the rain. The stage is days late. Aside from the chicken, Ruby has potatoes boiling and biscuits cooling. My stomach grumbles, knowing we're going to miss out.

"You saw the bounty hunter?" I ask Ruby.

A smile plays on her lips. "You mean Chord?" She clucks her tongue, "Can't say I have. Supper will be on the table in another hour."

"It smells good, but Mr. Davenport has invited us to dine over at the hotel."

Ruby wipes her hands on a cloth on the counter. "You'll be wanting to get into your dress again. I am sure Chord can help you. I can't leave the kitchen with these potatoes boiling."

Heat rises up my neck. Last time the bounty hunter helped me into my dress, it got us hitched! Then my mind goes down a track I tried to close off. What cowgirl can forget a kiss like the one he planted on me in the hotel?

"But I haven't seen him," Ruby says, beaming. Her eyes twinkle, and I know she can see the kiss replaying in my mind. There is no chance for it to happen again. The bounty says what he means, and our marriage is in name only. He was married before, and it's part of his secret what happened to his wife. Deep down, I have a feeling it wasn't good.

"Maybe I'll check with the sheriff."

"To help you in your dress?" She looks aghast.

"To find the bounty hunter."

Slowly she smiles. "The sheriff will be stopping in for supper tonight. You can ask him then." Ruby goes back to check on her potatoes. Come to think of it, Ruby has on a new dress. Under her cooking apron, she's wearing a deep burgundy red, dark as the wine they serve at the hotel. Her hair is neatly twisted, with wisps hanging over her perspiring forehead. Her cheeks are rosy. It's nice walking into the warmth, to the smells, to a familiar face.

Waiting for the sheriff would make me late. There is more I need to find out if I'm going to solve Coose's murder before the good sheriff of Deadwood sends Conway upriver.

Thinking of rivers, the gambler's voice sounds down the hall. He's staying at the boarding house, too.

"I'd best be off."

"I would offer you one of my skirts, but I'm still curvier than you."

Ruby looks after me like a mother hen. All these years, she and Pearl have taken to making sure I could cook, sew, and have basic education and manners. My mother ran off and left me with Earl. Now, she's back and thinks she deserves a piece of the claim Earl and I had. My father may have made a big mistake by gambling our claim and trying to marry me off to the gambler, but he did one thing right. He put my name on the deed instead of Polly's.

"Mr. Davenport will have to get used to seeing a woman in pants," I say. "Who needs a dress for eating dinner?" It's ridiculous how these Easterners are coming out here with their fancy ways.

"Did I hear someone say dinner?" the gambler sticks his head through the open doorway. He's hair appears a shade darker, hiding the red highlights I have secretly admired. Some would consider the gambler dashing, but I won't ever admit it to him. Men like the gambler take compliments as a personal stroke against their ego. Way too intimate, but I've got a husband.

He's a hard man to find. The bounty hunter is always on the move. I used to keep my window open for him. Now that we're married, I see no sense. He can come through the door if he wants to come to my room—our room.

Ruby informs the gambler that dinner will be ready in an hour.

"Shall we take a walk?" the gambler holds his arm out for me.

Ruby answers on my behalf. "Jo needs to find her husband. They're having dinner with Mr. Davenport this evening."

"Excellent." The gambler claps his hands together. "It will be a good opportunity to discuss current events with him." The gambler wiggles his brows at me. "He might have some information to help us clear Mr. Conway's good name."

I tell Ruby about agreeing to help find the actual killer. "Mr. Conway swears he is innocent. The bounty hunter believes him."

"And you?" Ruby asks.

"For his sake and mine, I hope he is." I don't say more in front of the gambler. I know he feels he has a stake in this, too, but he's the reason I need the bounty on Coose's killer. I have the deputy as a witness to Conway's word to pay up should we clear him.

"Shall I wait for you to dress for dinner, darlin'? Mr. Davenport likes his pre-dinner drinks promptly at five."

Ruby presses her lips together, leaving me on my own with the gambler. "I should find the —," I catch myself and say, "my husband."

"Shouldn't he find you?" the gambler shakes his head. "My dear Jolene, as flattering as we men find it to have women chase us, a man should always know where his wife is. Seeing Mr. Townes has lost one wife, it disappoints me he keeps little track of the one he has now."

"You make me sound like a child or a horse in the stables." Pulling back my shoulders, I say, "My husband and I have an agreement. We trust each other. We don't need to be stuck together at the hip."

"Shame." The gambler follows me down the hallway. "If you were my wife, I'd never let you out of sight. The last thing I'd want is some other man trying to steal her away."

"What makes you think another man can?"

Then comes the grin and the dimples. My insides flutter as those emerald eyes darken, their gaze locked on mine. The last time the gambler tried to get fresh with me, I clocked him. That thought alone puts an ache in my hand and dissipates everything else.

"Well, then, you won't mind if I accompany you to dinner. I'm sure your husband won't mind since I saw him riding out of town earlier."

The bounty hunter left town. Without me? Why that.....

Taking a deep breath, I stop worrying. The last thing I need is for the gambler to see he's struck a chord inside me, not my husband Chord, and not the kind to make a girl's knees weak.

As I head to the door, the gambler clears his throat. "While

I'd love nothing more than to see you strutting around in your trousers, Mr. Davenport is a less conventional man. We need him to talk."

I hate to admit it, but the gambler is right. We've got slim to no suspects. Not bothering to correct him, I glance at the stairs and then back at the door.

Stepping into the formal dining room, I spot the grandfather clock Ruby keeps in the far corner. It ticks away the seconds. If I hurry, I can visit Pearl. Maybe Ella Mae left a dress I can borrow that doesn't require a torture device to wear. Grace might have one, but I don't have any money, and I'm not about to ask the bounty hunter to buy me another dress. I'm broke thanks to the land dispute and my late father's gambling habit.

Out the door, the gambler trails behind me. Moisture clings to the air. Someone should tell mother earth to ease up. All this water will flood the gulch if it doesn't stop soon.

There are puddles in the road. Mud covers the boardwalk around the shops on main street. Ruby's place is one of the original homes the town has expanded around. I lengthen my stride, determined to get to Pearl's place quickly.

"You go on. I can make it where I'm going fine."

"Mr. Davenport won't like it if you don't show," the gambler warns.

"You're the one who insisted I needed a dress. Go on." I try to wave him away.

"No offense, darlin', but I'll accompany you where you're going. It's not safe for a woman to walk around this town alone. Too many strangers coming in and people dying."

My hat dangles down my back. I keep it there for when I need it. Setting it on my head, fixing my chords, I sigh. For a second, the gambler's eyes soften, and I think he might care for me.

He just doesn't want me to die because then the bounty

hunter would inherit my share of the land. "I hardly think anyone's gonna shot me headed for the reverend's house."

The gambler pulls out his pocket watch, flips it open, and looks at the time. "I like the way you think."

"Such as?"

"Skip the wooing and head straight for the vows. First, we'll have to get the paperwork straightened out with the church and the judge." He matches my strides.

"I'm not marrying you. I have a husband."

"In name only," he points out, a little too smugly.

"Some people like to get to know each other better." I take a step off the boardwalk and splash in the mud. It hits the gambler's pant leg. Darn. Mr. Fancy Pants might have to go change his clothes before supper. He shakes a leg and keeps on walking.

"Ha! You admit it!"

"When you admit you're only doing this for the money."

His hand flies up to his heart. "Darlin', you wound me."

"You're lucky I don't have my shotgun," I tell him. "Now scoot, I've got business with the reverend's wife, and it doesn't involve you."

Thank goodness he takes a hint.

Pearl and two of Ella Mae's sisters are in the kitchen. The others are working on their homework for school the next day in the living room. Little Lizzy whines about doing her times table. She's lucky she's got a momma and a schoolteacher to help her learn them.

"I'm glad you stopped in," Pearl welcomes me with open arms, but I can see the lines pulling down her face. Rose, one of Ella Mae's sisters, sets the table. Without Ella Mae there, Rose can move to the family table for meals.

"I wondered if I could borrow a dress, maybe one from Ella Mae," I wince, saying her name. Rose pauses, and even their other sister Lizzy looks over from the other room.

Pearl takes me by the arm, leading me to the stairs. "Of course. I have been meaning to stop by the boarding house. You're still there with your husband, right?"

I nod.

"I altered the yellow dress, but I'm sure Ella Mae will be happy to share." Inside the room Ella Mae once shared with her sisters, Pearl opens a chest. Most of Ella Mae's things are there. Pearl whispers, "Have you seen her?"

"Not since the hotel and the incident."

"Incident?" Pearl doesn't know. She settles on the bed, a dress in her hands as I tell her about the murder at the hotel and Ella Mae's distress. Pearl clutches the dress. "When you see her, you'll tell her she can come to get her things anytime, and she can visit. I understand, and I forgive her."

Not wanting to get in the middle of a family affair, I know Peral cares about all the girls. I promise should I see Ella Mae, I'll give her the world. Chances of Ella Mae coming back to town, if Lincoln took her to the ranch, are slim I'll see her anytime soon.

"You take the yellow dress and this skirt," Pearl pulls out from me. It's black. I wonder if Pearl thinks I'm headed for a funeral. "Here are shoes." She pulls a pair from the trunk, but those fancy heels aren't too practical. The look on her face guilts me into taking the shoes, the skirt, and the dress, all bundled in my arms. Hurrying to get back to the boarding house, I spot Reverend Carter riding down the street on his sorrel-colored mare.

The man is a force to be reckoned with, but I suppose saving souls isn't a calling for the softest hearts in a town like Deadwood. Although I seem to recall Ella Mae once telling me, we are all God's children, and if Ella Mae and Lincoln are married in the eyes of the Lord, then surely Reverend Carter, like his wife, can forgive Ella Mae for wanting a husband and family.

I can't help but wonder if I'll do the same. Long ago, I decided I wouldn't ever be like my mother. Who knows if I'll get that chance? What kind of life would I offer a child if I can't secure my land? Besides, I'm old enough to know it takes two to tango, and the bounty hunter hasn't asked me to dance.

What had Coose said to Daphne to make her react as she did? I never thought to ask. Did he have someone back where he came from? A wife? Kids? Who else would have wanted him dead?

8

Hardly a soul remains in the hotel dining room when I enter. The gambler greets me first. His smile doesn't reach his eyes. There's still no sight of the bounty hunter. I asked Ruby to tell him where I'd gone. With no time to fuss about what to wear, I opted for the yellow dress. Pearl did a fine job, adding another layer to the skirt front. It's lighter than the original, and she added ivory lace. It's a beautiful vee at the bottom to keep my cowgirl boots from showing. Last time I wore it, some ladies in town had a good time pointing out my boots were showing.

Best thing about it—no torture device required.

The grey clouds have brought a chill to the evening. Ruby lent me a wrap. It matches the black heeled shoes Pearl lent me of Ella Mae's. They're in good enough shape for one of her sisters to wear, and guilt sways me to wear them. So far, the heels are a little unnerving, and they pinch my toes in the front. Wobbling a little, the gambler comes to my aid, offering his arm. Where was he as I stumbled my way here?

"Why look at you." Daphne raises a brow with a pout on her lips. "What is this? You've got a husband, and you've hooked Mr. Weston with your attention? I do say, please share."

The gambler chuckles. "It would delight me to escort both you ladies to dinner." He holds out his arm for Daphne. Her face lights up as she takes his other arm. Ignoring the sly look on her face, we head to the small bar in the dining area. With the Saloon boarded up, Warner has not hesitated to make accommodations for the patrons to come over to the hotel. There are a few choice characters with a shot of whiskey in their hands.

"May I get you, ladies, a drink?" The gambler asks. Daphne requests a glass of white wine. Before I can answer, the gambler says, "Don't worry, darlin', I know what you like." He winks, turning for the bar.

"You can't be satisfied with one, can you?" Daphne fluffs her hair. She's left it down tonight, the black glinting with almost a blue hue in the lights of the lanterns. "I thought we had an agreement, Jo-Dee."

"You'll get your man," I assure her, uncertain who that man will be. She never mentioned who her father chose for a husband. It couldn't have been Coose. He's dead, and she's still after my gambler.

I've got to stop thinking of him this way.

"Good." She tilts her head and smiles. Mr. Davenport stands near the bar with Mr. Harris.

"I see you took some of my advice." Daphne steps back to inspect my appearance. My shawl has slid down my back and hangs from the bend of my arms. She motions with her hand, and I tug at my skirt to show her I've got on the black heeled boots. "It's a start. We will have to do something about your taste in fashion." She wrinkles her nose at the panel insert Pearl made at the bottom. "But it's creative. I'll give you that." She shrugs. "Do tell. Where is your husband this evening?"

Biting the inside of my cheek, I hesitate to admit I don't

know. Soon, the gambler returns with a glass of sherry for me and a glass of bourbon in his other hand. Mr. Harris isn't far behind him and hands Daphne a glass of white wine. "Thank you."

Warner plays host in the dining room, showing a couple to a table on the other end of the room. It's not something a hotel owner does, but since I came to town, Warner has surprised me with all the things he does in his hotel to keep it running.

Rain drizzles down the windows. Fat drops run down in streams.

"Tell me, Mr. Harris, are you staying in town long?"

"As long as it takes for us to see the railroad come through," he says, looking at Daphne. She avoids him, moving closer to the gambler. She lays her hand on his arm and tries to pull him into a conversation.

"I would have thought you'd have to return to the crew. You are the foreman, aren't you? And with Mr. Conway in jail and Mr. Coose dead, who will oversee the track coming through?"

Mr. Harris pulls at his tie. "Nothing is coming through until we dig into the mountains. Coose has cost us more than time. Tried to convince Conway to change the route but he insists coming through the mountain cuts travel time."

"Why is that?" I ask.

"Not safe coming through the open plains. Makes it vulnerable to attack. The mountains are the best bet. Coose should have done his job. Now, my men are camped in the hills waiting for word to move forward."

"Let me guess, there's one plot of land holding you up."

Harris holds out his drink in acknowledgment before taking a long swig.

Taking a sip of my own to hide the smile playing on my lips, knowing what piece of land indeed. I glance over at the gambler. As if on cue, he steps away from Daphne and places his arm around me. His hand on my back sends an unwelcome warmth into my spine.

Daphne crosses an arm under her bosom and takes a drink of her wine. Tonight she has on a lovely lavender gown, one I've seen her in since we first met. Diamonds are winking from her ears and one at her throat.

Mr. Harris can't seem to take his eyes off her diamonds, especially the one dangling right above the valley of her cleavage.

"Well, I'm not at all sorry Loose is dead. Even my father said he was incompetent."

"You mean Coose, not Louse," I say.

"Oh, no, I mean Louse. It's what I call him. The man was a Louse. Thomas, I mean Mr. Conway, complained to my father all the time about him. Didn't he, Mr. Harris?"

Mr. Harris shifted his weight to his other leg. He wore a gun belt, simple with a worn handled army handgun. "I don't believe Lloyd's failings are an appropriate discussion for a lady, Miss Davenport. I will, however, say the man was part, Cheyenne. He knew these hills and the people who lived in them."

Taking another sip of my sherry, I notice how Mr. Harris looks at me. "You said Coose wanted to change the route?"

"He suggested it, but I can't say more than that. It's rail-road business."

Or he wouldn't speak of it because I was a woman. I glance over at the gambler, tilt my head, and he leans closer. "I believe Mr. Harris needs another drink." I whisper.

"Of course," he holds up his glass, "Another Gilbert?"

"Call me Bert, and I could use another."

The gambler moves away, and I motion for Daphne to follow. She's slow to take a hint, but then Mr. Davenport signals for us to join him, calling out Daphne's name.

She rolls her eyes as her father holds out his hand in wait

for her. He doesn't act like a man trying to marry off his daughter. No, more like Reverend Carter, whose daughters have to run away to get hitched. It strikes me. What if Daphne wants to get away from her father and the marriage bit is made up? There are better options in town than the gambler.

But that's for another time. I have to remember why I agreed to dinner in the first place. "That's an army-issued weapon, is it not, Mr. Harris?" I ask, "Were you in the calvary?"

His hand goes to his weapon. "You know guns, Mrs. Townes?"

"It's Jo, and I've seen a few. My father had an old sawed-off shotgun, and we had a few neighbors that would pass through, some of them with the calvary."

"I was. Served many a year at Fort Davis. Then I got shot and nearly died. They let me go home."

"And you started working for Mr. Conway?"

"I am a man that believes in progress."

"They allowed you to keep your weapon?"

"We have to purchase our own. A man is only as good as the gun he carries. Your husband is a bounty hunter, is he not?"

"Yes."

"I believe he would agree with me."

"Probably," I say. "Did you know Mr. Coose before the railroad?"

"He was a scout then, too. The calvary let him go to help the railroad. I don't like to speak ill of the dead, Mrs. Townes, but Lloyd had a bad reputation when it came to women and following orders."

"I suppose he didn't have a wife then?"

"Doubt it, but he used to talk about a woman, Black Bird, Raven, something." Mr. Harris shrugs. "He'd mention it when drunk, and I say this to you because I know you're not as delicate as Miss Davenport. You haven't been sheltered. Your husband is a lucky man to find a woman with some grit. This is hard country, and it takes strong people to survive."

"Which is why you can understand I won't be letting go of my land easily. My father and I worked hard to build what we have."

Mr. Harris scratches his head. "No offense, Ma'am, but from what I saw, there's nothing but a giant rock and a shack no better than the lodges I've seen the natives build."

"Careful, Bert. Jolene may seem tough on the outside, but she's still a woman and sensitive to the insults of condoning the place she calls home. Mind you, I've hoped these past weeks we've been able to keep her in civilization would influence her to stay here in town."

"I mean no offense," Mr. Harris takes the offered drink from the gambler. "I suppose we should all take a seat for dinner."

With his hand pressed against my lower back, the gambler pauses before going to the table. His other hand has become empty, and I wonder what he has done with this drink. He takes my hand. "Jolene, I appreciate you allowing me the pleasure of your company this evening."

Bringing my hand closer to his lips, my breath catches. Those deep green eyes never leave mine. He kisses the top of my hand. I bite my lip when a warm body presses against mine. The gambler's hand drops from my back. The deep rumbling voice of the bounty hunter sends every nerve ending in my body on alert. "And I'd appreciate it if you kindly take your hands and lips off my wife."

Pulling my hand out of the gambler's grasp, I press it to my stomach to stop it from flipping.

"Of course," the gambler steps away, "I was merely keeping Jolene company in your absence."

Behind me, I can feel the bounty hunter stiffen. He keeps

his chest pressed against my back until the gambler leaves to join the others. "Next time, wait until I get back."

"Seeing as I didn't know where you were, and I was told you were last seen riding out of town, I didn't want to miss this opportunity to speak with Mr. Davenport. I didn't know Mr. Harris would be here."

"Who told you I was out of town? Weston?"

Sighing, I glance over at him as he comes around beside me. "Does it matter?"

His jaw ticks.

"Yes, it was him."

"I don't like him interfering. He's up to something."

"I couldn't agree more." He slips my hand around his arm. He sheds his long jacket, but his gun hugs his thigh. There is mud on his boots and the bottom of his pants.

"You should have told me about the supper plans instead of Ruby."

"You should have told me where you were going so I could find you."

Those grey eyes turn to stone. "We should take a seat. They're waiting for us."

All eyes are watching and waiting for us to join the table.

"I found out some things," I say.

"We'll talk about them after dinner."

"Are you coming to my room?"

His gaze stays on the gambler. "It's our room," he says, "And I might."

I press a hand to my belly, knowing I won't be able to eat a bite of dinner.

At the table, I take a seat beside Mr. Harris, leaving a space for the bounty hunter beside Mr. Davenport. As the bounty hunter pushes in my chair, he whispers in my ear, "You look nice, but I still like the green one better."

Get your head out of the clouds, Jo. Soon, the bounty hunter will move on, and who knows if he'll dissolve this marriage once the land dispute is settled. I've got a killer to find and a bounty to collect. I'm nowhere closer to solving Coose's murder than I am at persuading my husband into another kiss.

9

With the saloon closed, the hotel grows crowded. All too soon, the bounty hunter has me by the arm and walks me home. I spot Polly standing between Mr. Davenport and Mr. Reed on our way out. I know she is up to something. She's been sticking around ever since she came to town. Judge Stevens granted the gambler the land instead of her. So, what is her game?

These darn heels aren't made for walking. I wobble on the walk. "Steady there," the bounty hunter smirks. It's a good look on him, with the shadows covering the side of his face. "Something happen to your boots?"

"Something wrong with the ones I got on?" Slowing down, I step carefully not to trip.

"Nope," says the bounty hunter. "Never took you for a town girl."

"And that means?"

We step down off the boardwalk, heading for Ruby's. Light glows from the window of the sheriff's office, and the cafe has closed for the night. Horses trot down the streets, with riders keeping their heads covered from the rain.

Pulling my shawl closer, the bounty hunter's body heat

makes me shiver. Lengthening his stride, I have no trouble keeping up until my heel catches, and I stumble forward. Without him catching me, I would have face planted right there in the mud.

Some men call down the street. They're none too happy to discover the salon is closed. I can't wait to get these heels off when we get to Ruby's. I stop inside, not caring as a wide-eyed older woman watches from the parlor with her grey-haired husband. I pluck at the laces and tug at my shoes. Holding onto the bounty hunter's arm to keep me steady, he frowns.

"Hold up." He takes back his arm as I hop around. My other heel catches on my skirt, propelling me back. Arms waving, yelping, my butt hits the floor, then my back.

Standing over me, the bounty hunter's lips press together, his eyes soften. Propped up on my elbows, I say, "Don't you dare laugh at me."

"Jo, are you okay? I thought I heard something." Ruby comes out of the living room with a book in hand.

"Fine." I ground my teeth, shoving down my skirt, so no one else gets a good look at my underwear. The bounty hunter crouches in front of me. He grabs my ankle and unties my shoe.

"What are you doing?"

Plucking at the laces, he says, "Getting these off before you kill yourself."

His hand stretches above my ankle, touching the exposed skin on my leg. Heat spreads up my neck as he yanks.

Grunting, the shoe comes loose, and he starts on the other.

"Young man, I believe you've come to the wrong place. There is a hotel and a saloon for this kind of behavior." Standing at the doorway of the parlor, the grey-haired old man wags his finger at the bounty hunter. Behind the older gentleman, the wife peeks around, her hand over her mouth.

My jaw drops. The bounty hunter makes quick work of my

other shoe. He tosses it over his shoulder, making a thud on the floor. "The lady is my wife." Grabbing me by both hands, he jerks me onto my stocking feet.

"They must have just got married. We should let them go on their way." The older woman pats the old man on the arm.

The bounty hunter tips back his hat and opens his long jacket to reveal his six-shooter.

Grabbing his hand, I tug him towards the stairs. "Come on, *husband*, it's time to go to our room."

He couldn't let it alone. The bounty hunter winks at the older woman as he follows me up the stairs.

At the top of the stairs, I release his hand. Shoving a hand in his pocket and another on his gun, he follows me to the door.

My hand rests on the knob. My heart skips a beat.

"Good night, Jo."

"You're not going to come in?" Disappointment lays heavy in my gut.

"It's late. I should go."

"We have suspects to discuss and unfinished business," I whisper. Footfalls sound on the stairs.

We wait. The sound comes down the hall. The bounty hunter stiffens. Turning the doorknob, I tug on his jacket, hoping he'll take the hint.

He steps forward before I can open the door. Wedged between his body and the door, his head tilts down. The sweet smell of tobacco hits me. His warm breath brushes against my cheek.

"What is this?" the gambler's voice causes my hand to slip, and the door flings open behind me. Falling back, the bounty hunter wraps his arm around my waist as I arch back.

"Bravo," the gambler claps his hands. "Shouldn't you save the embraces for the other side of the door? Unless you wanted to be caught. You don't have to pretend for my sake." The gambler waves the pair of heeled boots in one hand. "Although you made quite the impression downstairs. Wish I'd been there to see those legs of yours, darlin'."

The bounty hunter's arm tightens. There is a tick in his jaw. "Watch what you say in front of the lady, Weston."

The bounty hunter pulls his jacket back further, his free hand going to his gun. My throat tightens.

"Jolene's not a delicate little flower, are you, darlin'?" The gambler grins, those dimples sinking into his cheeks. The flash of his teeth puts me on edge. He won't have his pretty smile for long if he keeps baiting the bounty hunter.

"Go inside the room, Jo."

"Ignore him, and let's go inside," I whisper. "We have better things to do than stand out here and amuse him."

"I believe I heard your mother say the same thing to the banker fellow when they came into the hotel after you left."

My fist curls into the bounty hunter's jacket. Heat flares over the tips of my ears. "If you're referring to Polly, she may have given birth to me, but she's not my mother. And what she does in her free time is no business of mine."

"It might, seeing how she offered to make a deal with me." My boots swing in his hand.

"What kind of deal?" the bounty hunter asks.

The gambler relaxes, dropping his hand with my boots. "The kind that would put the saloon back in business."

"Glen is in jail." A torrent of emotions churns inside me. How many times do I have to be reminded my father is dead?

"But he's not dead," the gambler rocks back on his heels.

The bounty hunter's hand remains around me and the other at his gun. He barely moves. My grip tightens on his leather jacket. "It's getting late. We should go to bed."

The grin on the gambler's face drops.

"You can hand those over. I appreciate you saving me the effort of fetching them in the morning."

The gambler tosses the boots at my feet. He backs away into the shadows of the hall. Sagging against the bounty hunter, I don't realize I was holding my breath until the gambler disappears.

The bounty hunter opens the door and gives me a nudge inside. Picking up my boots, he joins me. My heart races as he shuts the door. Light from the moon cuts a dim light across the center of the enormous bed.

One by one, my heeled shoes hit the floor near the dressing screen. Ruby added the screen the day after the judge declared the bounty hunter and me married.

He paces over to the nightstand, lifting the glass of the lantern. A match strikes the wood, and he lights the wick. Reaching inside his pocket, he pulls out a cigar. Using the lantern's flame, he lights it, then puts the glass back over the flame. Light flares inside the room.

Moving over to the window, he opens it enough to let his cigar smoke curl out. With his back to me, he stares out the window.

Silence stretches between us.

"What do you think Weston meant?"

The bounty hunter takes another draw from his cigar. He angles his face away from the light. He's got several more years under his belt, and I imagine much more experience than me in these kinds of matters.

"Don't worry about it. Like you said, it's none of our business what Polly Dean does or Weston."

"I don't trust them." It's honest to God's truth. Since Glen killed my father, I've trusted two people — Ella Mae and the bounty hunter. I shouldn't trust him. He's got secrets, but he knows what I'm hiding in the mountain and why it's crucial for me to get the other half of my land back. There's nothing in it for the bounty hunter except the ten percent I promised him. Since he's my husband, the law puts him in control of my half of the land. I haven't been able to figure out his motive.

"You shouldn't."

My instincts have never led me astray, and my gut tells me Chord Townes is one of the good guys.

"Even you?" I ask.

He takes a long draw on his cigar, turning his head to blow smoke out the window. "Especially me.'

Silence fills the space between us. There are so many things I want to ask him. A feeling overcomes me to reach out and touch him, but I stop, unsure how he keeps his back to me. His eyes reflect the darkness from the other side of the window and the light within.

Those eyes are haunting.

Standing there in the middle of the room unnerves me. I head for the screen in the corner where I tossed my pants and shirt from earlier. There's a chair behind it with a nightgown hanging from the back.

"Where did you go? Did you find something new out about who might have shot Coose?"

Up on the mountain, I usually slept in my clothes. You never knew when you'd have to jump up in the middle of the night to chase off some wild creature or run from Earl in one of his firewater induced moods.

"Not any more than you did. Next time we get an invitation for dinner, don't accept unless you talk with me first."

Biting the inside of my lip, I touch the lace on the nightgown. Ruby gave me this nightgown when I first came here. It has lace around the collar and down on the hem.

"I talked with Daphne earlier. I don't think she did it, but she thinks Conway did it to protect her."

"He thinks she shot him. It's possible," he says.

"I can't see Daphne shooting someone, even if he was a bit lude with her."

I feel the bounty hunter's eyes on my shadow from behind the screen. Never a shy one, I drop the yellow dress to the floor. Like the shoes, I can't stand wearing it any longer.

"Then it doesn't leave us with many suspects."

"What about Harris?"

"He was with the others."

Stepping out from around the screen, I flinch when his chin raises, and his eyes meet mine through the mirror of the window. Trying not to let his hooded look tie me in a dozen knots, I move over to the bed and sit, tucking my legs beneath me.

"We need to find out if he made anyone else mad in town. I was hoping Mr. Davenport would have given us some information to help, but you're the one who talked to him."

"Davenport is worried about his investment. He's dropped every dime he has into the endeavor."

Reaching up, I tug at my curls in thought. "He'd need money to marry off Daphne, wouldn't he? Don't them rich folk expect a dowery or something?"

"Out east, maybe."

"If a woman has to pay a man to marry her, she shouldn't bother getting married."

"Is that so?" He snuffs his cigar out on the window seal. Ruby won't be happy with the ashes or smudge.

"Who needs a family, anyway?" Grumbling, I tug on the lace of my nightgown. Back home, I would run in nothing more than my skivvies in the summer, along with Chitto and the other children in Tail Feather's tribe. Their sense of modesty differed from the ways of the folk in town. As I grew long-legged, Earl brought me home a pair of pants and told me to always keep covered.

The bounty hunter remained silent for much longer than usual. My heart sank, realizing what I said and seeing the pain etched on his face. Jumping off the bed, I reach for him. The bounty hunter pushes up the window. He swings a leg through the opening.

"Chord," I say, and he looks at me.

A faint smile forms as he says, "Sleep well, Dimples. I'll see you tomorrow."

He reaches for the tree.

"Wait!"

He pauses.

"Won't people talk if they don't see you coming through the door in the morning?"

The gambler and his promise to get my marriage annulled play in my mind. Plus, without Shorty, my sawed-off shotgun, I don't feel safe with another killer out there.

"Go to sleep, Dimples. You'll need it if we head out tomorrow to track a killer."

Before I can ask where we're going, he's gone. Standing at the window, watching him slip down the tree and disappear into the shadows, my insides freeze.

Instead of the breeze outside sucking the smell of his cigar out, I find it blowing in my face. Like the bounty hunter slipping into the night, someone slipped in and killed Lloyd Coose. But who?

Crawling into bed, I realize, too, the bounty hunter got away again without telling me the agreement he has with Davenport and Conway. I suppose I'll have to find out from the railroad man or investor. My days are numbered, and Tail Feathers and his people have no idea the railroad is coming. I'll have to find a way to warn them right after I figure out a way to clear Conway's name.

10

On Sunday, the church folk are somber. While I sit between Ruby and the bounty hunter, Ella Mae and Lincoln are nowhere to be found. My heart aches. I miss her and the time wasting away before I leave and who knows when I will come back to town. Once I've got my land back and return to the plot of land I call home in the mountains.

Usually, folks pray for rain this time of year, but Reverend Carter leads us through the last prayer, asking God to stop the rain. Outside the church is a wet, muddy mess, and the folk are tired of this weather. They're not the only ones, as Lottie Larson and Hannah Baker approach us after service. People don't seem to hurry outside this morning as they usually do. Hannah wears a dark bonnet and Lottie her blue gingham dress.

"I'm so glad we caught you before you went back home," Hannah says. "We were wondering if you'd mind putting together a picnic lunch for the May Festival in a couple of weeks. We're having an auction to help raise funds to build a courthouse right here in Deadwood."

"A courthouse?" Ruby presses her hand to the middle of

her chest. She's got on a wool skirt and long-sleeved blouse with a matching black jacket. Seems this morning, the weather has got everyone down. The black skirt Pearl lent me of Ella's Mae's fits snugly, but it's warm and goes with my blouse. Taking the bounty hunter's advice, I wore my cowgirl boots. They're way more practical for a girl to slosh down the street with all this mud. I even kept my petticoat clean.

"With Deadwood expanding as it is," Hannah explains, "We'll need a place for the judges on the circuit to come without disturbing the children's school day. Why, with the railroad building a station here on the other side of town, we might get a judge in residence."

"We wouldn't have to ship off the criminals to Silver Valley," Lottie adds.

The bounty hunter stays silent.

"Mrs. Thompson is making her pies, and we're asking all the single ladies to prepare baskets," Hannah looks at me, her lips pouting. "I'm sorry, you won't be able to contribute. After all, we wouldn't want you being seen eating out with another man since you are a married woman."

"Are you suggesting Jo has been in the company of other men?" Ruby tilts up her chin.

"Who am I to gossip?" Hannah smiles, giving Lottie a sidelong glance. The other woman plays with the ribbon of her bonnet.

The bounty hunter's eyes narrow.

"There is Miss Cravat and Miss Parrish. They traveled here on the stage before the rain hit. They're on their way to Crooked Creek to meet husbands. Perhaps, since they are here and staying at my boarding house, you might talk them into participating in the fundraiser. Of course, they may leave before then." Ruby pointed them out. Hannah and Lottie move quickly through the crowds to reach them before they can exit.

Relief radiates from me as I feel the bounty hunter relax.

"Pay them no mind," Ruby says, taking up the bounty hunter's arm on one side and I on the other. "They should focus more on finding husbands of their own than ogling yours."

Daring a glance at the bounty hunter, his face remains unchanged. He had to have heard her, but he ducks his head against the rain. His long leather duster keeps him dry while Ruby pulls her jacket tight. I put my hat on, not carrying what anyone might have thought in church, as it dangles down my back by the neck strings. This weather has made my curls go flat. It hangs over my shoulder in my favorite braided style.

Not as many folks showed up for the sermon. Halfway back to Ruby's, the sheriff catches up with us. He tries to persuade Ruby into going to the cafe for lunch with him or the hotel. "I've got Sunday dinner to prepare," she insists. "You'll join us, won't you? I'm making a sweet potatoes pie for dessert."

Ruby once told me the way to a man's heart was through his stomach. I think she might be right. Sheriff Bentely can't contain his glee. Sweet potato pie must be a favorite of his. I make a mental note to ask the bounty hunter about his favorite food.

There is so much I don't know about him.

Back at the boarding house, Ruby goes to work in the kitchen. We spend a good part of the afternoon peeling potatoes and basting ham. Mr. Clark sits in the parlor, a chess game sits on the table, and the older man from the night before says, "checkmate." The older woman sits in a chair near the window, with Miss Parrish across from her. "Mrs. Townes, would you like to join us?" They're both crocheting lace. I shake my head, "Sock knitting is about as far as my string talent goes."

"We'll teach you," Miss Parrish holds up her work. Those small, dainty loops feel intimidating.

"Have you tried booties, dear?" the older woman asks. My

cheeks flame. There is no way to turn it off as frequently as it keeps happening.

"Maybe someday," my answer appeases her. "If you'll excuse me, I should find my husband."

"She might need those booties sooner than later," I hear the old woman say. Good thing me, and Ella Mae are the only ones who know my marriage is in name only. And the gambler, too. How can I forget him?

At what lengths would he go to get my marriage dissolved? Zings of giddiness erupt under my skin. What woman doesn't want to have a man trying for her attention?

Sadly, the man who vies for my attention isn't my husband. Shaking my head, I try not to think about the way the bounty hunter kissed me at the hotel or the way he held me against the doorway.

He told me not to trust him.

My gut tells me he's lying — about more things than one. Perhaps after finding Coose's killer, I should find out who I married. But a promise is a promise. He doesn't reveal my secret. I don't ask about his.

I'll have to find a way around our deal to dig into his secrets. Starting with the agreement he made with Davenport and Conway. Deep down, I have a bad feeling about all this.

Walking through the downstairs, there is no sign of the bounty hunter. Two other men sit and play cards in the living room while another man flips through the pages of the Sunday edition of the newspaper.

Heading to my room, I don't find him there either. How will we ever catch the killer if he keeps taking off on me?

In the past few days, Ruby has taken on a few more boarders. As a result, every room in the house is full. Tension brews in the air right along with Ruby's coffee. It's heady, and if I don't watch myself, I'll get caught in the charades going on in the living room.

Everyone has become stir crazy, and I can't blame them. We've all asked for the rain to stop in our nightly prayers. It's been a constant drizzle. In the evenings, Mr. Clark sits by the fireplace in Ruby's living room, telling stories of his homeland. His voice and the fire cozy up to a girl at night. No one says anything to me about my missing husband.

Ruby has a mile-long list she needs from the mercantile, so I volunteer to go for her. Miles has gone off to the telegram office, and the elderly couple residing at the boarding house to wait for the stagecoach to arrive. Most of the new boarders are from the hotel. Word of Coose's death frightened a few of the guests.

On my way to the mercantile, I go by the sheriff's office. Peering in the window, I spot Deputy Payne looking up at another figure on the other side of the desk. It's hard to make out the other person's face. Who would hang out at the sheriff's office this early in the morning?

Walking past the window and about to glance back to see if I can identify the other man, I run smack into a body.

"Good gracious!" Polly wobbles back, and I reach out on instinct. She grabs my wrist, her eyes wild and her hair a mess. Even under the hat, it flies in every which direction. "Watch where you are going!"

Wanting nothing more than to bite back the apology on my lips, I can't. Pearl and Ruby taught me better, even if the woman abandoned me. "Sorry," I mutter.

"That's better." She pulls her shawl tighter around her. The air is damp and cool, thanks to the never-ending drizzle. "What you looking at, anyway?"

Biting my tongue, I try to go past her. She's the last person I want to be around. "Think you're too good to give a woman a simple greeting in passing? You might not like who I am, but I'm still your mother."

"You're standing in my way," I try to step around her.

"I'm not the only one, honey buns. You still trying to find the killer to free the railroad man?"

"That's none of your business."

She drops a shoulder and presses her lips out in thought. She hasn't changed since my childhood memories. Although I don't remember her wearing dark colors or daring dresses.

"I am not gonna give up. I'm going to get my share. It's best you, and I pair up. Word has it there are people who might get in your way."

"The gambler," I grunt, stepping down on the street into the mud to avoid Polly. As soon as I can get past, I jump back on the boardwalk again. A wagon slogs through town, and a few riders come in, shoulders hunch together with their hats down, to beat off the drizzling rain.

"He's got his eye on you!" Polly chases after me.

"I'm married." In name only, but if the kiss I shared with the bounty hunter in the hotel is any indication, I'd say the bounty hunter likes me. My neck warms, and I flip up the collar of my shirt. The air isn't cold, but the misty rain chills a body walking through it for a while. I left my warm winter coat at our cabin in the mountains.

Hopefully, the mercantile will have one, and I have enough credit left to pay for it. Ruby's list propels me forward.

"Darlin'," Polly mimics the gambler. "If you haven't done the deed, then honeybun, your marriage isn't legal."

"Says who?" I want to slap my hand over my mouth at my blunder. "What's it anyone's business? We're married. What we do at night isn't nobody's concern." I grit my teeth to keep them from chattering and to keep from saying anything else I might regret.

Polly laughs. "You have to keep a man in your room long enough, honey buns, to get him in the marriage bed."

Almost to the mercantile. I halt, and she catches up. She's got a twinkle in those eyes as she leans in, saying. "Do you know where your husband goes every night? Because I do."

My jaw unhinges. He wouldn't! Would he?

Narrowing my gaze on Polly, she frowns. "Oh, honey bun, do you need me to tell you? The wife is the last to know. It's why we need to stick together, you and me. You can't trust anyone. We get that land, and you won't have to worry about your man. He can take as many bathes as he wants, and you can do whatever you want. We could start a business right here in town."

I go from cold to hot in seconds. My chest tightens. My gut twists. Reaching out, I grab a pole under the roof of the saloon. At first, Polly continues to pity me, but then she lays a hand on me. "Jolene. Are you okay, honey buns? We'd best get you inside somewhere."

Shaking my head, I launch off from the pole.

"Let me help you."

"I think you've helped me enough."

Marching into the mercantile, Lottie Larson and another woman are by the fabric and notions. They pause from their conversation. Robbie ducks out from around the counter. Slapping down the list, I tell him to fill the order and deliver it to Ruby. If only I had a nickel to my name, I could pay the boy for his extra effort.

Marching back out, I pass Polly again. "What you are you standing there gawking at?"

Her eyes widen, and she steps away from me.

Lottie and the other woman peer out the window from inside the mercantile. My ears are burning, my chest squeezing. Who else in town knows?

Polly follows behind me. Jumping off the boardwalk into

the muddy street, I don't figure Polly will keep up. She rushes down the walk as I head toward Swanson's mansion. It's a good distance walk.

My fist clench and unclench. Why should I care? The bounty hunter did me a favor. Our marriage is in name only. The gambler has suspected it. Ella Mae let it slip about our fake marriage. When he kissed me, it didn't feel contrived. I know it has all been a show, but if Polly knows, and the gambler knows, and Ella Mae knows.. who else knows?

Bursting through the door of the Swanson's mansion, no one is in the foyer. At the end of the stairs, a sleepy-eyed woman yawns as she comes down the stairs. Blinking, she tilts her head to scowl at me.

"Which room is he in?"

She shakes her head.

"Townes. Chord Townes. Where is he?" Marching closer to her, the woman cowers. I knock my hat back.

"Haven't ever heard of him." She scurries off to another room.

I head up the stairs. The main bathing room is downstairs, but I know there are private rooms upstairs. As I top the landing and spot the woman who once helped me with my hair. Her name is Minnie, but she doesn't see me. She's carrying a stack of clothes. Outside the door, she goes in. I hear his voice.

My stomach bottoms. Knowing I should turn around and go about my business, I can't. The kettle has blown. Up the stairs, someone approaches. Did Polly follow me here? Maybe it's one of the girls working at the bathhouse. Or maybe it's one of the Swanson sisters. I don't care.

My curiosity will be the death of me.

At the next sound of his voice, something inside me snaps. Patience was never one of my strong suits.

Not bothering to knock, I swing open the door and catch

him in the act. Minnie stands beside him, helping him put on his shirt. One sleeve and his back are exposed. My breath catches in my throat. Thick white slashes run down his skin. My hands cover my mouth.

The surprise on the bounty hunter's face when he glances back turns to a scowl. Pushing Minnie away, he turns and finishes putting on his shirt. Standing there, shirt open, he says, "Jo...."

My nostrils flare. My hand curls into a fist in my mouth. Those grey eyes of his go light as ice. Minnie hurries toward me, but I've seen enough.

Turning on my heel, I rush back down the hall, down the stairs. "You can't come in here whenever you want!" a woman yells.

Outside, Polly heads in my direction. I take off toward the boarding house. Someone calls my name.

There is no burning off this mad. As soon as I reach the boarding house, the gambler comes down the stairs. Pushing past him, I run for my room.

He calls my name.

Inside my room, I grab what meager belongings I have. It's not much. I realize I have nothing. The green and yellow dresses hang over the screen and my nightgown. None of them belong to me. The green dress with flowers came from the bounty hunter. I'll forever think of it as my wedding dress.

The photo of Polly, my father, always kept staring back at me from the mirror above the water pitcher on the stand. I toss it on the floor.

Heading down the stairs, I brush past the gambler again. "Darlin'?"

Inside the kitchen, Ruby tosses another set of sheets down in a tub of water. With all the rain lately, she's been hanging them through the house to dry.

"I need my gun."

Her head snaps up.

"Ruby, give me my gun," I say, calming down for the first time since finding the bounty hunter at the bathhouse.

"You got my supplies?" She looks around me to where the gambler ambles down the hall.

"Robbie is delivering them. I need Shorty, Ruby. Give me my gun so I can go."

"You should wait for Chord if you're going after someone. You don't want to bring in the wrong man."

"I don't need the bounty hunter."

"I think she means to shoot him," the gambler snickers, leaning against the wall outside the kitchen.

Ruby's cheeks flush from washing bedding. Her eyes round out as another strand of hair slips from her bun. "What are you going to do?"

"Give me my gun so I can go," I say, the heat of my mad cooling to build a dam behind my eyes.

"You're leaving?" Ruby wipes her hands on her apron.

"I've got a killer to find."

"Where's Chord?" she asks.

I bite the inside of my cheek, glancing back at the gambler, and Ruby takes the hint.

"Give me a moment."

Crossing my arms, I wait. Ruby takes her time leaving the room. She doesn't allow anyone to know where she stashes the guns she confiscates.

Behind me, body heat and the smell of old paper and rose surround me.

"Trouble in paradise, darlin'?"

"Go away," I say.

"We can go see Mr. Osterloh or ride over to Silver Valley to find the judge and dissolve this. You don't have to commit murder to escape your husband."

Whirling around, the gambler spreads out his arms. His

emerald eyes shine with concern. "It'll be alright, darlin'. Just you wait and see. Everything always comes back around the way it should have been."

Backing away from him, Ruby returns. Hesitantly, she holds out Shorty, my sawed-off shotgun.

"You sure you need this?"

Shorty makes me feel safe. There is no other way to explain it. If I'm to hunt down and find Coose's killer, I'll need the one thing I can trust.

Polly was right about one thing. You can't depend on a man.

11

The bounty hunter warned me not to trust him, but I'm no fool. My days are running out, and I'm no closer to figuring out who else could have taken out Coose. Why?

It swirls in my mind as I head for the stables. Someone calls my name, or maybe it's the man slowing his wagon saying 'whoa' instead of 'Jo.' Either way, I don't care. I need to see Ella Mae. She always has a way of helping me rationalize things. Maybe she can help me figure out what I've missed to help Coose and get the reward money to save my land.

"I need my horse."

Hank rolls up his sleeves, and sweat trickles down his face. The forge at the end of the barn licks with flames. He doesn't bother looking at me. "Out back in the corral."

"How much do I owe you?"

"Still got your wagon, don't I?"

With Shorty in my hand, I leave the barn. The corral is around the back of the stables. As I near the corner, I trip, and Shorty goes down first. Face planted in the mud, I take a moment to get my breath and peel away from the ground's suction.

"You hear that?" a voice asks.

"Probably one of the horses in the barn."

They sound familiar. Retrieving Shorty, I swipe the mud off. Covered from head to toe in slimy muck, I huff.

Then I hear, "Just make sure you keep your end of the deal."

Inching closer, I sneak a peek around the barn. Reed Campbell? What's he doing out back here with... is that Mr. Harris?

"I want my money," Harris says.

Reed's back is to me, picking up his feet as they sink further into the mud. "You'll get your money when the deal is done."

"That wasn't part of our—."

"Jo!"

Reed turns, and I duck back. The bounty hunter carries his gun belt in his hands. His shirt is half-buttoned, and his hat tipped forward. Those eyes are as hard as his expression. My grip tightens on Shorty.

The bounty hunter steps forward. I take two back. His shoulders pull back. Wrapping his gun belt around his waist, there is danger in the way he glares at me.

"What did you think you were doing?" It comes out more of a growl than anything.

The two men are no longer behind me. Several of the horses look over at us. I whistle for Lulu, she knickers in response. Why on earth Hank would send her outside to trot around in this mud, I'll never know.

As the bounty hunter descends toward me, my heart takes off since my legs won't. "Why don't you go back to the bath-house? I'm sure someone lost the soap and needs you to track it."

For a moment, the bounty hunter goes still. His hand poised at the buckle of his gun belt. My breath hitches. Shorty feels heavy in my hand.

Laughter spills from the bounty hunter's mouth. His deep chuckle scares some horses, even my Lulu spooks at the sound.

"What are you laughing at?" Ears burning, cheeks flaming, and words at the tip of my tongue no cowgirl should let loose, my legs unlock, and I take off toward my horse.

"You!" He bellows with laughter.

"You're the one who's humiliating me!" Pointing to my chest, my hand slaps on the mud sliding down over my clothes. I glance down.

"Oh." I touch my face.

The bounty hunter stops laughing. Those grey eyes of his darken. Seeing him all clean, the vee parting of his shirt at his neck sends a knot in my chest. Grabbing the wooden corral fence, I try to heave over it. My leg doesn't quite make it, and I miss the mark.

"What are you trying to do?" He asks from behind me.

"Get my horse and get out of here."

"You're not going to find the killer up in those mountains," the bounty hunter hangs back.

"No, but I'm not gonna stay here, so you can humiliate me." It hurt. I am not sure which part more: the fact he married me in name only or the fact I don't feel good enough to measure up to the wife he once had. The whole town didn't need to know it.

After another attempt to go over the fence, I decide to go between it. Putting Shorty's butt in the mud, I bend to go through and figure out the sisters and I won't both fit.

"Is that so?" the bounty hunter says.

"Yeah, that's so!" I don't mean to shout, but I am halfway through the gap between the corral and not able to wiggle my way through. So, I grab Shorty at the same time the bounty hunter grabs my gun by the barrel. We lock gazes.

"Let me help you before you go getting hurt."

Why do people keep saying that to me? Yanking the gun,

the bounty hunter yanks back. "Go away. I don't need you, your name, or your help!"

"Whoa there, Dimples."

Too late, I slide between the rails, end up on my shoulder, and scramble to right myself. My rear end greets the bounty hunter. Giving me a shove, my behind catches up with my front end, leaving Shorty behind. Lucky me, my hand still has a hold of Shorty, and the bounty hunter's hand slips over mine.

"No, you whoa there. Let go of my gun. I got places to go."

"You're mad."

"You think?"

He refuses to let go of the gun, his warmth over my cold one. A shiver slips down my spine, or maybe it's the mud going down my pants.

"You saw my scars," As I scramble to my knees, my arm suspends through the rails holding onto Shorty, my body freezes. "Is that all you're worried about?"

His brows furrow.

It comes out sounding heartless. My expression softens, and my fingers go lax on Shorty. "I don't care about your secrets." Okay, maybe I do. "And you're not the only one with scars." I've seen a few. I've got one on my thigh in a hunting accident with Chitto and some of the other young warriors. Chitto nearly killed Yellow Cat for hurting me. Earl would have killed me if he knew where I'd gone traipsing off.

"You shouldn't have come barging in. What were you doing there?"

"Polly told me," I tighten my grip on Shorty again. "The gambler knew, too. He's got no problem helping me dissolve our marriage. He knows it's fake. They all do."

My chin wobbles. The sting of tears comes on suddenly. I'm embarrassed, but deep down, there's more to it. I like the bounty hunter; he makes my blood sing when we're close.

Except I'm too filled with confusing emotions, I can't

differentiate between them. One moment I'm mad as a hornet, the next sorry and guilty. It's not my place to push his buttons. He'll share his secrets when he feels he can trust me.

Neither one of us is there yet.

Living in the mountains, I know better than to let my guard down. The bounty hunter was there when my father got murdered. He was there to save me and capture Glen, the man who killed Earl. The bounty hunter also saved me from the gambler by marrying me.

He didn't do any of those things to help me. How could I not be grateful?

Trying to pull Shorty away, I say, "Thank you."

Shock flashes across his face.

"If the gambler had both halves of my land, he would have sold it by now. I know I'm not really your wife, and whatever happened to your last one is your business. You can sleep at the bathhouse all you want, hang out at the saloon, or ride off. I don't care. I've got a murder to solve."

Behind me, Lulu has made her way over. She presses her head into my back and rubs, shoving me against the wooden rails. My hand releases on Shorty, and the bounty hunter takes it out of reach.

"You're not going to get far on your own."

Shooing Lulu away, I get to my feet. "Well, I can't trust you, now can I?"

Slowly he raises, a few inches taller with his hat. His eyes hood, and the rain falls heavier. "That makes two of us."

From behind, Lulu nods her head. The rain makes her snort. Patting her slick mane, the feeling is mutual.

"I'll take my gun back." I hold out my hand.

"Not unless you want to roll in the mud again."

"Are those fighting words Bounty Hunter?"

"Come over that fence, Mrs. Townes, and find out."

A shiver goes down my back. This time, I'm certain it's not the mud or the rain. The sultry look he has makes me shiver.

"I think it's time we have that talk." Walking over, he opens the gate. His brow raised.

All this time, the gate had been right beside me. Turning, I give Lulu a pat. It doesn't hurt for her to be out prancing in this rain. She's a mountain pony used to the outdoors.

The bounty hunter keeps Shorty for safekeeping on the other side of the gate.

"Right after we get you a bath."

I follow the bounty hunter back to Ruby's with my head hanging low. She takes one look at me and declares it will take more than a basin of warm water to find the cowgirl beneath the mud.

The bounty hunter helps carry the tub into my room. Meanwhile, I help Ruby heat the water. She made me go out back to come inside and kick off my boots on the porch first.

Once the tub is in place, the bounty hunter helps carry in the buckets of water. Soon as the tub fills, I shed my clothes for Ruby to take. I hear the door click as she leaves and sinks further into the water.

Bathing is a luxury. The hot water seeps into my cold bones. Sighing, I grab the soap and get the mud off my face.

"Let me know when you're ready to rinse."

The soap slips from my hand, landing on the other side of the tub. "I'm bathing. What are you doing in here?"

The tub sits in the corner behind a screen.

"We need to talk."

"We can talk downstairs. Does anyone know you're up here?" I sink further into the water, glancing around for the sheet to dry off. I haven't even washed my hair.

"Don't you want them to know I'm here? Isn't that what got you riled earlier?"

Keeping my arm across the sisters, I reach to find the soap. "No looking."

"Not even a shadow," he says, which makes me think he can see my outline from the sunlight in the window coming through the screen.

"Turn around. Your back better be towards me."

"Don't worry, Dimples, you're safe with me." Says the man who told me not to trust him. I believe him, though. Why else would he avoid staying in our room now that we're married? The bounty hunter is a mystery, one I will have to solve eventually.

Funny thing is, I've never cared or been this shy before. Growing up around Chitto and the other members of Tail Feathers tribe, modesty wasn't an issue. Thinking of those summer days wading in the creek makes me long to return.

"Start talking," I soak up the heat and take my time in this luxury.

"It's not what you think," he says.

Wrapping my hands around the soap, I lather up. "Give it to me straight."

"Minnie is an old friend."

Whose room he happen to be in? Trying not to let the jealous monster rise, I divert him before he can say more. The man doesn't want to talk about the past, but he'll tell me about a night at Swanson's with the woman who did my hair.

"What's up with Davenport and Conway? What aren't you telling me?"

There's a creek in the bedsprings as I imagine him getting comfortable. "It doesn't matter. With Conway in jail, nothing will move forward."

"You admit you have something going on between the three of you?" I lift my leg out of the tub to soap it up.

"They made me an offer, Dimples. I didn't...."

His voice trails off for a moment, then he resumes and says, "Davenport is pushing for the tracks to go through."

I put my leg back down in the water. "Daphne told me. He's got a lot riding on this. He's even set her up with a suitor. She is so desperate she's chasing the gambler."

"Weston."

"She thinks Conway thinks she did it and is covering for her, but I don't know why he'd do that."

"He's..." then his voice drifts off at the same time as I raise my other leg to wash it. The bounty hunter can't see through the screen, right?

"He's her father's business partner. The man's a good decade older than her. He's probably looking out for her like an uncle. She went to the jail to see him. Don't know as I would do that if they suspected me of murder." The soap keeps slipping through my fingers. I lower my leg as the soap plops back into the water. I reach forward and try to find it.

"Women do unpredictable things when they're afraid of getting caught."

If he says more, I don't hear him. I slide down into the tub and get my hair wet. As I go down, my legs go up.

"Legs again," the bounty hunter mutters loud enough for me to hear him. My face turns as flushed as the rest of me from the warm water. It's been cooling fast, and I speed up getting my hair washed.

"The sheriff is looking into things a little deeper. Things don't add up. Conway admitted he paid Coose to scout and persuade the landowners to sell. He got paid extra on the side."

"Bribed, you mean," I huff and dig my fingers into the tangled mess of my wet locks.

"There has been tension between Davenport and Conway. With Conway out of the picture, Davenport has the lead to run things."

"He's made Harris his right-hand man," I say.

"He approached me and offered me Coose's job." The bounty hunter's voice sounds strained. It made sense now. Davenport and Conway need a man who can use a gun.

"I wonder if Davenport knows Harris is making deals with Reed?" I tell him about what I heard around the barn.

"You ready for a rinse? Your water has to have gotten cool."

"You offering to help me out, Bounty Hunter?"

The bed creaks again. His boots hit the floor. He reaches around the screen, the bucket in hand, tipping toward me. I shriek a little, "Forward more. You'll spill it on the floor."

"Here." He leans the bucket forward more, stretching and keeping his face and body on the other side from view.

"Easy."

He tips the bucket. A waterfall pours down, and I angle my head beneath it. It's lukewarm, making me shiver as I get the suds from my hair. As soon as the bucket is empty, he's gone.

I wipe the water from my eyes.

"What do you think Reed has to do with this?" I wring the extra water from my hair.

The bounty hunter hasn't moved. I see the shadow of his frame against the screen.

"Harris could have a side deal. I'll see what I can find out from Reed. Harris likes to gamble at the hotel in the evenings. He's taken Conway's seat at the nightly game."

"How do you know about that?" I reach for the sheet. My fingertips brush the edge.

"Invite from Davenport."

I rock back and forth, not wanting to rise from the tub. The water has turned brown from the mud.

"I didn't take you for a poker player." Almost, I stretch and lean.

"There's a lot about me you don't know, Dimples."

"You play with them?" I snatch the sheet and pull up, but the tub tilts. Instead of going back, it comes forward.

"Every night."

"Night?" My voice pitches as the tub betray me. Forward I go, the tub thumps over, water spills, and the screen crashes over. The bounty hunter isn't as close as I thought. He jumps out of the way, and there I am, like a fish on the bank flopping out of the water. The sheet lies beneath me. Soaked. The upturned tub covers my butt.

"Jo, you, okay?" The bounty hunter wades through the water on the floor, getting the rug soaked under the bed. He helps me up, the wet sheet clinging in my hands, draping between us.

Searching for words, he gives me a hooded look. A draft comes behind me, and I shiver. His hands are on my arms. My mouth parts as he pushes back a piece of wet hair from my cheek. It puts those funny little zings guiding over my skin.

"Anyone ever tell you you're a handful?"

Hearing those words makes my heart race. "I'll clean this up."

Someone bangs on the door, making me jump. "Jo? Jo? What's going on in there?"

The bounty hunter grabs the quilt from the bed and drops it over my shoulders as the door bursts open.

"So much for locking the door."

The gambler comes through the door, his hand on his shoulder where he slammed against it. Behind him, Ruby and a few others staying at the boarding house peer inside.

As I turn, the bounty hunter pulls me against his broad chest. He keeps me covered as I bury my face in his shoulder.

"What's going on in here?" Ruby pushes past the gambler.

"Oh…"

I look as she gasps.

"You better hope this doesn't drip down through my ceiling, Chord, or you'll be patching it, you hear?" She says it sternly, but there is mirth in her eyes as I turn my head to see the crestfallen expression of the gambler.

"Understood." The bounty hunter tucks me closer. My hands go to his gun belt.

"I'll go get a mop and some towels." Ruby rushes out, but the gambler stays.

"Mind, Weston, my wife and I were in the middle of a bath." The bounty hunter tilts his head against mine.

"In the middle of the day?" the gambler scowls, making me almost feel bad for him.

"Jo was a dirty girl."

My jaw drops. I bury my face again so the gambler can't see the flames crawling up my neck, hitting my cheeks, and scold the tip of my ears.

"What are you doing?" I hiss.

"You wanted others to know this is real, didn't you?" He whispers in my ear.

"Yes, but not like this."

He chuckles, planting a kiss on my shoulder. His eyes narrow on the gambler, the bounty hunter's arms tighten around me. I grab the ends of the blanket, pulling it between us.

"When you're done playing games with this hired killer, darlin', you know where I am."

Moments later, the rock facade of my husband relaxes. He crosses the room, heading out the door to meet Ruby with the mop and towels. I scramble for clothes.

I can't help feeling I've ruined more than my clothes. If it weren't for me being a married woman, my reputation might be on the line. There can't be any doubt about my marriage, but why does seeing the gambler's scowl make me doubt?

Deception has a way of complicating things and leaving behind dead bodies.

12

It took hours to clean up the mess in my room. The rug hangs out back under the porch to dry. The mattress on the bed managed to escape the flood in my room. The bounty hunter leaves me with the mop while he deals with the damage downstairs.

Ruby kicks us out, and the bounty hunter splurges for a room at the hotel. When things dry out, and her ceiling in the living room is repaired, she'll let us return.

The bounty hunter can't escape through the window or sneak out to stay somewhere else. He disappears for most of the night and comes back to the room while I sleep. I found him on the bed beside me, above the covers, and fully dressed this morning. His hat covers his face, and his hand lies beside his gun.

Not that I should be surprised. A man in the bounty hunter's profession would have to sleep with one eye open and his gun within reach. I'm tempted to tip his hat to see if he is asleep. The gentle snores are enough validation for me.

Checking my braid, I fling it behind my back. My clothes were stained, and Ruby refused to give them back. With no choice, I fiddle around with the corset. There has got to be a better way for a woman to get dressed. No wonder they all need husbands. You need one to tie these contraptions. Glancing over my shoulder, I can't come to wake the bounty hunter. His finger is to close the gun, and I don't want to be dead before breakfast.

Thanks to the tub fiasco, the sisters are just as happy inside the green floral dress, and my cowboy boots are as good as clean. My hat managed to survive, and thank you, Lord, it's dry.

The room is a bit stuffy for my liking. There isn't much space between the bed, the amour, and the washstand. Our room has one window with the brown curtains drawn shut. Carrying my boots until I get out into the hall. As I emerge as man goes by, his brow raised.

With a hand on the wall, I slip my feet into my boots and keep on walking. Down in the lobby, Sherman dares to glance at me. He wouldn't even look at me when the bounty hunter brought me in. Warner gave us a room on the same floor with Davenport and the rest of the railroad big wigs staying in town. Conway's room is at the end, but it's locked, and the bounty hunter said the sheriff had already searched it.

With no money to buy breakfast, I head over to Ruby's. At the boarding house, breakfast is included with the monthly rate the bounty hunter pays to keep his room reserved.

Surprisingly, there's not a drop of rain coming down. The clouds are all but invisible in the pale sky.

Deadwood is in a gulch at the base of the mountains. It's like a giant bowel keeping all the water in. Too bad it doesn't keep the vermin out.

On my way to the boarding house, I spot Mr. Reed on his way to the bank with Polly at his heels. Ducking my head, I keep walking. No doubt she and the gambler are in cahoots to take my land from me. Polly should know better. She lived on our claim. Doesn't she remember who our neighbors are?

A woman who would abandon her child and leave her husband without a second glance doesn't care about anyone else.

Inside the boarding house, I can smell the bacon and the coffee from upstairs in my room. Ruby has a full house, and I feel guilty leaving her in the kitchen. She's got the biscuits and gravy on the sideboard, and the bacon disappears as soon as she gets it on the plate. There's a hot pot of porridge and warm bread. She must have run out of eggs.

Those chickens in her backyard can't keep up with the demands of a full house. I take my coffee, glancing around as I add a splash of cream. Humming as I take a sip, my belly growls at both the sight of the food and the full table in the dining room.

Taking a biscuit and a piece of bacon, and my coffee, I retreat to the kitchen. It's heaven in grease in there, along with the scent of another custard of Ruby's making.

"One of these days, you'll have to teach me to make egg custard," I say, leaning against the counter in the middle of the kitchen. With a house as big as this, it has to have an enormous kitchen. The cherry wood and brick near the stove make me wish I would have a home as sturdy as this one day.

The gambler once talked of white picket fences, but he's not the type. Mr. Fancy Pants, aka the gambler, is a man on the move. The only thing holding him to this town is the prospect of getting hold of my land and selling it for a profit.

Humming as I take another sip of coffee, Ruby says, "You'll have to find me some eggs first. My poor hens are about clucked out with this crowd. Normally, I get a full house around the May Festival, but it's still a good two weeks away."

Two weeks seems like a lot of time for some, but for me, it's a ticking clock to find Coose's murderer.

"I'm not complaining," Ruby wipes back another strand of her dark hair. She's been showing more white streaks of late when she pulls it back. She keeps it in a tight bun with strands escaping as she works.

"I've had to turn a few folks away who wanted to leave the hotel after the murder."

"Who would have thought a dead man would be good for business?" I stuff my mouth with the last of my biscuit as Ruby points her wooden spoon at me.

"Did you find out anything more about the murder? Benjamin said Judge Stevens would come back around for the festival. Everything is pointing toward Mr. Conway's guilt. I don't suppose you and Chord have come up with any other suspects?"

"Benjamin?" Having been in town for a few weeks now, I can't recall anyone with the name.

Ruby's blush is as rare as a mountain rose. Flustered, she huffs, picking up the porridge and carrying it to the dining room. Not about to let her get away, I follow her with my coffee.

"Why Sheriff Bentley, of course," she puts down the porridge and steps out of the way. As I get a good look at her, she's pale, except for the pink across her cheeks.

As long as I've known her, I've never heard her call a man by his first name as casually as she does Bentely. She refers to the bounty hunter by his first name. Few do. I figure it's because he lives here, renting a room each month for God knows how long. I sure don't.

When she speaks of him, it's in a motherly way. She does the same with me. But the sheriff?

I smile into my coffee. Ruby's gone all sweet on the sheriff.

"You should take him breakfast," I suggest.

She waves me away. "I already invited him anytime." She

wipes at the sweat on her brow. "Before all these boarders came. You got time to make another run to Jensen's?"

"I can drop off the list for you again." After that, I need to visit the bank. One can hope Polly has finished with her business for the morning with Reed by the time I get there.

"I'll give you some money. I need to pay on my account. All these supplies lately, I'm sure my credit has run out." She pats down her dress, looking for a pocket.

"You should charge for all this food you're cooking and maybe hire some help."

"Then they'll go to the hotel, the diner, or the cafe." She taps her finger against her hip.

"The hotel charges. You give both breakfast and dinner. Maybe you should provide one or the other. You're one person feeding a small tribe."

Maybe I shouldn't have used the word tribe. Ruby narrows an eye on me. "You looking to help? You have a murderer to find and a knack for getting into trouble."

I gulp down the rest of my coffee, closing my eyes for a second to savor the sweet taste of the cream. I never knew coffee could taste this good.

"It was nice when you were helping me." She sounds deflated. "I suppose I should consider hiring help or charging more."

"Or both," I say. "I'll help when I can, but I'm not planning on staying here."

"Where do you think you're going, Dimples?" My spine straightens at the sound of the bounty hunter's voice.

He walks further into the dining room. For a moment, I contemplate slipping back into the kitchen. Then I spy something in his hand.

A few boarders head for the porridge. It's standing room only. As he comes near me, a sea of people part for him. Several of them frown, and a few do a double take.

He holds up my corset. "Forget something?"

My eyes go wide. I reach for the corset, but he holds it up and out of reach. "What are you doing with that?" I whisper fiercely.

Ruby chuckles and grabs a biscuit, watching with amusement.

The elderly couple at the table has their eyes glued our way. The woman's face is incredulous while the old man eats to hide the laughter shining in his eyes.

"More importantly, what are you doing without it?"

I try to snatch it again and manage to get a hold of it, bringing it down out of sight. The bounty hunter keeps a grip on it.

"I can't put it on myself," I hiss.

"You could have asked me."

"And got shot for waking you up?" I glare back at him.

Behind us, someone says, "Heard those folk up in the mountains were a wild bunch."

Another says, "Wouldn't mind taming one myself."

My jaw unhinges.

The bounty hunter grins, his eyes hood, but those grey irises have darkened beneath them.

"The last thing I would ever do is harm my wife," he says with such conviction that it settles deep into my bones. I know he means it. The bounty hunter once had a wife before me. He doesn't talk about what happened. There's a pain in his eyes. It fades as fast as it appears.

"Good luck with that one," a man in a green jacket slaps the bounty hunter on the back.

"It's about time someone makes a proper wife out of you." Ruby clucks her tongue and heads back to the kitchen. "Don't you forget about my ceiling, Chord."

"As soon as it's dry." His eyes never left mine.

"Come on, Dimples, let's get you properly dressed."

"I'll show you where." Ruby leads us into the kitchen.

"We can't go up to our room?" I ask.

She points to the pantry. Her deep frown reminds me she's still sore about the tub incident.

"It's dark." And a small space. I'm not a fan of either. Having once been trapped in the mines while helping my father, the childhood fear never completely went away.

"You won't be there long."

As the bounty hunter presses me towards the pantry, my body trembles.

"Hey," he says softly, "You, okay?"

He steps forward, making me step back into the pantry. "I don't like tight, enclosed places."

He pulls the door shut. My body goes cold with sweat. "Easy, Dimples. We'll do this quick. Turn around and close your eyes."

"I don't like the dark either," I whisper. Something about the bounty hunter has me confessing all my deep, dark secrets. First, I told him about Tail Feathers and his tribe on our claim. He figured it out when I asked him to take up supplies my father promised the chief. They were getting antsy with me stuck here in town, trying to find my father's murderer.

The bounty hunter promised to keep my secret. This is one more he'll have to keep a lid on. I can't say the same for keeping his. He never shares with me. Someday, I'll learn to keep my mouth shut and out of trouble.

He strokes my shoulders, and I take in a deep breath. "You need to slip this down so I can slip the corset over your head."

Holding my breath, button by button, the top of the dress peels down. I've got a chemise on underneath, keeping my back and the sisters from exposure.

"Raise your arms."

A warm curl starts in my belly. Slowly, I do as I'm told. Bumps prickle my flesh as he slides the corset down over. Once it's down over the sisters in the proper place, he says, "Breath, Jo, there's no passing out until after I've cinched you up."

Did the bounty hunter try to make a joke?

"Relax. Put your arms down."

As I do, my lungs let go, and I breathe again.

He smells of sweet tobacco and something bitter on his breath. It's too early in the morning to drink anything but coffee. My arms cross around the front as he tugs on the back.

My body tenses.

"Still got your eyes closed?"

"Yes," it comes out breathlessly, and rightly so, as he tugs on those torture sting behind me.

"Almost done."

I can feel his breath against my exposed neck. He pushes my braid up over my shoulder. Squeezing my eyes shut, I try to think of anything and everything to distract me from where we are. Someone built a fire in here. My skin turns hot, and I pant to keep cool.

"When I was a kid, my dad would take me out with him on cattle drives. Every night, I'd lay as far from the fire as possible."

"Because you were afraid?" I ask.

"No. I wasn't afraid. The best time to see the stars is at night. The darker, the better. They shine brightest at night. I'd lay and count them until I fell asleep."

"Oh," I breathe.

His hand comes around my waist. "You can put pull the rest of your dress up."

I pull it up, fumble with the buttons, and turn around. "I can't see to do my buttons."

He reaches back and leaves in a sliver of light. His finger-tips brush mine. With the light, my body relaxes, and the cold dread gives way to the warmth brewing in my blood.

We're halfway done with my buttons when the door yanks

open.

Once more, I find myself covered by the bounty hunter.

"If last night wasn't enough," the gambler exclaims. "You are taking this much too far, Townes."

The muscle in the bounty hunter's jaw jumps as he grinds his teeth. He doesn't look behind him. Hurriedly, I fumble and rush to get my buttons finished.

The bounty hunter stays my hand. "You mind, Weston? My wife and I were having a moment."

The gambler snorts. "You hear him, darlin'? First in the foyer, then up in your room, now this? The man has no morals. I'd never put you in a position of promiscuity."

I lunge toward him, but the bounty hunter catches me and holds me back. "What happens in our room is private."

"He stayed with you last night, darlin'? The game went late last night. Heard you were staying at the hotel, but here you are."

The bounty hunter's fist clenches. I place my hand over it. "I want to punch him, too," I whisper.

Chuckling, the bounty hunter leads me out of the pantry. My entire body goes lax against him. His arm never leaving my waist, I press my hand to his chest.

The gambler glowers at us.

"Mr. Weston, breakfast is in the dining room. If you want some, I'd get it before it's gone," Ruby calls.

He points his finger at us, his mouth open about to say something, then he grins, showing off those dimples, and leaves us alone.

He's not the only one. When I look over at the bounty hunter, he's got a thoughtful look on his face. His eyes travel down over the dress.

"What?"

That stone facade returns. "We'll have to make a stop on the way."

13

For once, the bounty hunter and I have the same thought. We cross the street to the bank, grateful the gambler hasn't tried to follow us.

Once inside, we wait for our turn. The clerk at the window takes a step back. The bounty hunter doesn't go anywhere without his long leather jacket. It makes him look more intimidating to the outlaws he hunts.

I know what's under the jacket. I've seen his scars, and he's seen my bare butt. Two hot spots flare on my cheeks. Not those ones! The ones on my face. I press the back of my cool hand to both. You would think after a while, I'd learn to stop blushing around the man.

"Have you got another reward?" the clerk asked.

"Not this time."

The bank clerk almost looks disappointed. He clasps his hands together. "A withdrawal? I'll need to see your bank book."

"We're here to speak with Mr. Reed," the bounty hunter says.

The bank clerk leans back, his gaze going to the closed door. "I believe he's in a meeting."

The clerk clears his throat. "Did you want to make an appointment? Or come back later?"

While the bounty hunter speaks with the bank clerk, I inch my way towards Reed's door.

"Miss? Mr. Reed is in a meeting," the clerk says again.

I nod, hearing a familiar voice behind the door, and it's not Reed's. There is no mistaking the high-pitched shrill. My heart gets stuck between beats. I listen again to be certain.

"Miss?" the clerk is torn between leaving his station and coming to the door.

"Jo?" The bounty hunter strides my way. I press my finger to my lips, putting my ear to the door.

"You shouldn't be doing that. Mr. Reed's meeting is private." The clerk moves towards me.

Turning the knob, I open the door at the next sound. Reed and my mother jump apart. He hurries to put distance between them, but Polly sits on the edge of his desk with her hair down.

"What is the meaning of this!" Reed shouts. "You can't barge into a man's office!"

"Private, huh?" I look at the clerk. He seems more scared than surprised.

The bounty hunter crosses his arms. "What now, Dimples?" he asks.

"I apologize. I thought I heard a woman scream. I wasn't thinking...."

"Oh, I screamed," Polly winked my way.

"Shush, woman," Reed straightens his collar. "Mrs. Dean, I will take your offer into consideration and let you know in a few days," Read says, getting back into business mode.

Slowly, Polly hopes off the desk, taking a bunch of papers with her. They flutter to the floor as she saunters our way. As she nears, she gathers her hair and twists it back up, pinning it in place with the pins she pulls from her bodice.

"You always did have a way of spoiling my fun." She finishes with her hair and places her hands on her hips. "If you weren't my son-in-law, I'd invite you to walk me home. Seeing as you won't be long, maybe I will anyway."

"I'll have to respectfully decline," the bounty hunter says.

She pouts for a moment. "Have it your way." Looking behind her, she says, "I'll be looking forward to seeing you again."

Reed races to pick up the papers.

"Whatever it is you're after, honey bun, you won't find it here." Polly runs her hand down the bounty hunter's arm. "You change your mind; my room is three doors down from Minnie's."

Hurriedly, I go to help Reed. Grasping one of the papers and another from the floor, I notice they're land deeds. Reed snatches them out of my hand quicker than a fox after a chicken. "Thank you."

"Sure thing," I stand beside the bounty hunter in the doorway. He gives me a questioning look, but I shake my head. With his hand on my back, he presses for me to go forward. I give him a sharp glance, and his hand falls away. He steps inside Reed's office without me.

"Since you're free, mind if I ask you a few questions."

Reed huffs, puts the papers into a drawer of his desk and slams it shut. "Those are confidential," he says, puffing out his chest, his eyes meeting the bounty hunter. They stare at each other for what feels like an hour in a few seconds. Finally, I close the door and say, "It's not our business what you do with Polly, but I hoped you might shed light on Lloyd Coose's murder."

The bank must have loaned some of the prospectors'

money for their claims. Why else would Reed have deeds on his desk for places in the Black Hills?

Reed breaks eye contact with the bounty hunter to look at me. "What would I know about the man's murder? Did you see me there when it happened?"

"You were downstairs in the dining room with the others?"

"Hardly," Reed takes a seat. "I didn't go to the hotel for the town celebration of your wedding. I have a bank to run, and sometimes business runs late."

The bank runs on a clock. Reed never opens before nine and always closes not a minute after five, except for Fridays when the cowboys and the prospectors come into town. It stays open two hours later.

I imagine Reed sitting at his desk, counting all the money in the bank safe each night to account for every penny each day.

"Sounds lonely." No wonder Polly has got her sights on the man. It must get lonely in the company of cold, hard cash.

On the other hand, I like to keep some of my gold nuggets buried. My father never trusted the bank. He spent it mostly on firewater, cheap women, and cards.

"I'm a businessman, Mrs. Townes. Time is money, and I'm in the business of investments and banking."

"We won't waste any more of your time," I say. "You must be extra busy these days with the railroad in town. Heard they started building a station near the mountains at the other end of town. With all those workers and people traveling, it must be exhausting to keep up with the preparations to secure the bank."

The bounty hunter stays quiet at my side. He tilts his head, listening.

"That is neither for me to discuss or comment on," Reed says, heading for the door.

"Isn't that why I saw you and Mr. Harris having a discussion by the stables?" I try to act innocent like Daphne does when she's with the gambler.

Reed hesitates long enough to notice before he reaches past us to open the door. Then he thinks the better of it. Looking at the bounty hunter, he says, "I see you haven't taught your wife her place yet."

My eyes go wide as saucers. My thumb tucks into my curled fingers the way the bounty hunter taught me to make a fist.

The bounty hunter doesn't falter as usual. "You didn't answer my wife's question."

"I don't have to answer to you or to her. You're not the sheriff, and I am not the one who shot the railroad scout. I believe the sheriff has got his man."

"Then why were you meeting with Mr. Harris?" I press, trying to let go of his earlier comment.

The bounty hunter moves, blocking Reed from opening the door to kick us out. Reed takes a step back, realizing he's not going to push the bounty hunter out.

"Why else do I meet with people, Mrs. Townes? I'm a bank. People are always asking for money."

"Harris wanted a loan?" the bounty hunter asked.

"Confidential information," Reed says.

"So confidential you couldn't meet in the bank?" I ask.

Reed whirls around and heads back to his desk. "The man caught me as I was returning from checking on my horse in the stables. Some people don't care to keep their business behind closed doors." The way Reed says it and pointedly looks at both of us makes me feel as if I'm the guilty one.

"Any idea who might want to frame Conway and kill Coose?" the bounty hunter asks.

"Frame him? Who else would have something to gain by the man's death?" Reed walks back behind his desk. "Are we finished here? Unless you came and want to discuss payment on your land, Mrs. Townes?"

I grimace at the reminder.

"We still got plenty of time," the bounty hunter says, opening the door and motioning for me to go first.

"Ten days," Reed says smugly.

I mutter outside the bank, "So that's how she knew."

The bounty hunter doesn't miss a beat. "You're not going to let that go?"

"It's already behind us," I assure him. "What do we do now? Find Harris?"

The bounty hunter shakes his head. "We need to get you some new clothes first, then we'll take a ride."

"I thought you liked my dress?" I ask mockingly.

"I do." The one corner of his lips lifts. "I can't be around all the time to help you into it or out," his voice lowers with his lashes. A dozen butterflies hatch in my stomach when he looks at me like that.

No matter how much I try to remind myself, this isn't an actual marriage. The bounty hunter is sure making things hard. Each time since the night of Coose's death when he kissed me, we've come close to doing the deed again. I guess because there was no one to put a show on for, he didn't need to lock his lips on mine.

"What are you thinking, Dimples?" he asks as we cross back onto the other side of the street.

"What makes you think I'm thinking anything?" I ask.

"You've got that look on your face."

"Because you know me so well, you can tell what my facial expressions mean?" I challenge him, a little irked at myself for letting my mind take me down a dead-end trail.

"You would make a terrible poker player, is all I'm saying." We stop in front of Grace's.

"I've already got two dresses; I don't need anymore.

Besides, if we're going to go for a ride, I can put my pants on." Hoping they are dry and the mud washed all out. Ruby took them from me, and I haven't seen them since.

"Don't count on it," he says, holding open the door into Grace's shop. Inside, a woman ties her brown bonnet. Beside her, a small child clings to her skirt. I've seen that baby before, once in the mercantile when the bounty hunter helped carry her groceries. Her smile widens at the sight of him.

"Perfect timing," Grace says. "What can I do for you?" She's wearing a grey gown with an apron over the top. The woman keeps her eyes on the bounty hunter as she leaves. He holds the door open for her, and I see her stumble outside as she looks at him.

My lips quirk, more amused than jealous. *Sorry, lady, this man is mine.* Taking a step back, I don't know where that came from.

"We need a riding skirt for Jo," the bounty hunter tells Grace, "And a blouse or two."

I give him a sidelong look. "I got a shirt and Ella Mae's black skirt."

Grace grabs her measuring tape. "You ever had any clothes of your own?"

"Sure, I have. I have got pants and a shirt I wear all the time. Nothing wrong with them." I cross my arms.

"You *had* a shirt and pants until you ruined them by rolling in the mud." The bounty hunter corrects.

"What do you mean, had?" I drop my arms.

Grace steps in front of me. "Hold still. I'll have her measured up in a few minutes, and we'll talk about fabric."

"Whatever you think is best. Riding skirt, blouse or two, and whatever she needs underneath," he talks to Grace as if I'm not standing right here. "I'll go get the horses. I want to reach our destination before nightfall."

Nightfall? "Where are we going?"

He's out the door before I can get an answer.

Grace walks around me, taking measurements. I have half a mind to walk out and follow the bounty hunter, but if I move an inch, Grace steps in front of me and reminds me to stay still. The longer I fidget, the longer it will take her.

Sighing, I give up and give in to her, wanting me to hold out my arms and wrap that rope around my waist.

Several weeks back, the gambler bought me a traveling dress. He figured we'd be married, and I'd need a lady's outfit to go on our honeymoon. He talked about Texas, and several times while he tried courting me, we'd play cards, and he would speak of a riverboat. I should have paid more attention, but my priorities were different back then.

I gave the traveling dress back to Grace, seeing how the gambler bought it on credit and hadn't squared up with Grace even after.

"I'll take me a week. There are a few dresses in front of you. Did you want to throw in a new dress for the May festival like the rest of the ladies coming into the shop?" she asks.

"I got this one. I'm good."

"I sold the navy traveling dress if you were wondering. A woman new to town bought it a week ago. Didn't bat a lash at the price," Grace says.

"I'm glad." I really am. The dress had a bustle in the back and a tight skirt that kept me from taking my usual stride. It was worst than the black heeled boots Pearl gave me of Ella Mae's.

"Blue's not an awful color on you," Grace continues as she writes measurements and sketches a skirt on the paper. "Green brings out your eyes. Although black will wear better," now she's talking to herself more than me.

"Am I done now?" I ask.

Her wheat-colored hair tucked back in a bun, she shakes her head at me. "I won't make it too frilly for you, Jo. I'll keep it simple. This way, it won't take so long to get it made. I think a black skirt and then a green blouse and maybe a blue one more feminine than the one I've seen you in."

"My other shirt is brown. There's nothing wrong with it."

She scrunches up her nose. 'You got it from the Mercantile. there is everything wrong about it."

Grace moves over to where she had fabric piled and draping by the wall. "Those are men's shirts. They aren't made to fit a woman's curves."

I'm not trying to flaunt them either, but she says, "You *do* want to keep your husband's attention, don't you?"

Then she pulls out a blue piece of fabric, light as the sky in the early hours of dawn. "I think this one, don't you?"

I think it will take more than a few pretty blouses and a skirt to hold the bounty hunter's attention. I'm not his wife, or at least, not the wife he wants.

It's best I remember my marriage is more of a partnership. The kiss may have been a one-time thing to seal the deal for folks in town, but finding Coose's killer has become my main priority.

Things could change in a few days, and Grace would have put all this effort in for nothing.

It's best not to get too excited. There is something fishy going on between Reed, Polly, and Harris. I can't help feeling it's connected with whoever killed Coose.

14

As soon as I stepped out of Grace's shop, the rain fell again. The bounty hunter came riding down the street on his big roan stallion. The horse's body paled in comparison to its dark head. A black mane and tail stood out against the speckling of red and grey in the horse's body. Beside him, Lulu, my painted pony with a saddle on her, trots.

Curious, I head towards them. The bounty hunter dismounts ties both horses to a hitching post, then jumps up on the boardwalk beside him.

The man has lithe moves to make a girl's inside wobble. No wonder the ladies in Deadwood couldn't keep their eyes off my husband. Tall, dark, handsome, the bounty hunter fits all those descriptions and more.

"We'll have to make do. Hank didn't have a sidesaddle."

"Aside what?" I ask, genuinely confused.

"A woman's saddle," the bounty hunter places his thumbs in his belt. "It's raining again. Grab a jacket, and we'll be off. The temperature will drop before we get back."

"Where are we going?" The bounty hunter didn't seem the kind to surprise a girl, but then again, our whole marriage dropped on my lap in a matter of moments. He's unpredictable, as he is dangerous.

"Out to the Triple D. You want to see the reverend's daughter, don't you?"

Maybe the bounty hunter has a kind streak in him, after all. "I've been worried about her."

"I know." He says it like he knows me so well, and maybe he does. He knows me better than I know him for sure. "Grab a coat. I'd like to get out there before dark. We'll have to stay the night, then ride back in the morning."

"Yes!" I jump on my toes. Before I can think of what I'm doing, I've got my arms around the bounty hunter's neck, and my lips land on his cheek. "You have no idea how stir crazy I've been to get out of this town, even for a little while. And to see Ella Mae..." my voice drifts off, feeling him tense around me. I jump back, afraid I've upset him. "I didn't mean to... I'm sorry."

I take several steps back. He grabs me by the arm, his expression unreadable. "Go get your jacket, Dimples. This will give me a chance to check in with the sheriff before we go."

The air's been a little breezy with the constant rain. I can't remember a spring where the rain lasted this long or the chill clung to the air. During the day, a girl could go around in nothing but her regular duds, but the bounty hunter was right. I'd need to grab a jacket or, in my case, borrow a shawl again from Ruby.

Looking at Lulu, my heart went out to my pony. She shook her head, looking perturbed at me, and I could almost hear my horse's thoughts. She has never worn a saddle before, and it makes me think how quick Hank or the bounty hunter has been to put one on her.

We'd both have to adjust for this ride. While I fetch the shawl, I'd inquire Ruby about my pants. Then riding out to the ranch wouldn't be so bad for one of us.

Heading toward Ruby's, the bounty hunter keeps me from going far. "The hotel's in the other direction."

Might as well put my big girl panties on and confess. "I'll have to go to Ruby's. She lent me the shawl I had been wearing. I'll get my pants too, then I can ride out to the ranch."

The bounty hunter gives me a long look, sweeping down my body to my feet and back. "You don't have a jacket."

"I left it at the homestead. We were making a two-day trip. The air was warm. I didn't need it." Nor did I need to explain myself to this man, but feel compelled, I did.

"Jensen should have something suitable. We'll have to have Grace add one to your order."

"Is there a problem with the way I dress?" It seems everyone is trying to dress me up and change how I am.

"Nothing wrong with a woman wearing pants, Dimples." His eyes hood, giving me that sultry look that sends another wave of heat through my insides. The man is going to be the death of me.

"Then why the dresses?" I wave my hand, indicating the one I'm wearing.

A quirk comes to the corner of his lips. The bounty hunter is slow to smile, and it's a rare and wondrous occasion to see when he does. "Because you look nice in it. A woman who wears pants should also have a dress or two. Nothing wrong with keeping her options open."

The man confuses me. One moment he sets me on fire, and the other, his words toss a cold bucket of mountain snow down over me. I'll never understand him. Nor will I give up trying. We're hitched, for the time being, and if the gambler has his way, he'll undo our judge-appointed nuptials.

He takes me by the arm, and we head to Jensen's mercantile. He tells me that we'll have to stop in and see the sheriff later.

Jensen's stock is low. He keeps more dry goods and supplies

than clothes. Most of what he has is for men. If not for the sisters, I could have fit into some of them fine, but I don't.

There are more strangers in town than I remember. Most of them are men from the railroad coming into town for supplies. As I try on another jacket the bounty hunter hands me, I hear a man in the store tell Jensen they have a camp on the eastern ridge of the mountains.

My skin prickles as the bounty hunter tugs on the jacket while I try to button it. The man goes on about how they're at a standstill once they hit the curve over the next pass. If the rain doesn't let up, it will take them another month, maybe three.

Everyone's been praying for this weather to stop. Forgive me, Lord, if I can see the blessing in keeping the railroad away from Standing Rock and my land where Tail Feathers and his tribe reside.

There's been enough bloodshed in town lately. We don't need any running down from the mountains.

The wool coat comes around the sisters with little room to spare. The deep brown matches the bounty hunter's leather duster. He wears his duster like a second skin.

While the bounty hunter moves to browse another shelf, I move toward Jensen. "I'll take this one. Put it on my tab, will you?"

A couple of weeks back, the gambler tried to use my credit on my account, leaving me with nothing. Thankfully, the bounty hunter made Jensen give me back my credit. A coat like this will put me in Jensen's debt again. Once I get Coose's killer behind bars, Conway will give me the bounty. I need to save the land, and I'll be able to return to the mountain. Jensen always allowed us months of credit in the past.

He pulls out his book and runs his finger down the column with my name. "You don't have enough to cover it," he says.

"You've always granted me credit before."

Jensen shakes his head. "Too many strangers coming and going now with the railroad. You pay, or you put it back."

I huff at him. "Fine. I don't need it," I say and take it off.

The bounty hunter presses his chest against my back, stopping my efforts. Reaching around me, he tosses a pair of gloves on the counter. "We'll take these, too."

"Cash. No credit," Jensen informs the bounty hunter of my credit balance. After the way the bounty hunter stepped in to fix my account, I don't blame Jensen for his edgy behavior around my husband.

Reaching in his pocket, the bounty hunter pulls out the amount Jensen quotes for the jacket and gloves. The bounty hunter instructs Jensen to grab a few cigars off the shelf behind him, and we're on our way. I make a mental note of how much I owe the bounty hunter. My debts keep adding up.

Outside, the bounty hunter makes me put on the gloves. They're a perfect fit. He slips the cigars into his shirt pocket as we head back toward our horses.

Robbie comes running down the sidewalk, nearly plowing the bounty hunter over. Chord takes the young boy by the shoulder to keep them both from toppling into the muddy street. "Whoa there. What's your hurry?"

"I've got to fetch the doctor. Someone killed Mr. Conway!" Robbie takes off again. The bounty hunter and I race for the sheriff's office.

They wouldn't need a doctor to declare Mr. Conway dead. Bursting inside the sheriff's office, a very shaken Ruby stands to the side. Her hands cover her mouth while the sheriff and the deputy are inside Conway's cell.

The bounty hunter heads for the cell while I check on Ruby. "You, okay?"

She nods, her eyes wide and on Conway.

"What happened?" I ask.

Her head turns, not a hair out of place, her chin wobbles. "I brought him breakfast."

"The sheriff?"

She nods. "And for the others, too."

I spy the basket on the sheriff's desk. Conway lies on the floor inside one of the cells, a biscuit near his hand and a puddle of coffee across the floor.

A man with a black bag rushes inside the sheriff's office, pushing Ruby and me aside. I huddle close to Ruby, putting my arm around her shoulder.

With the doctor in the cell, they push the deputy out. The bounty hunter stays close to the desk, looking at the basket.

Deputy Payne struts over to Ruby. "Don't even think about leaving," he says.

My eyes narrow as Ruby trembles.

"She poisoned him," Deputy Payne explains. "She brought in all this food. It's a good thing the sheriff and I didn't take a bite of it."

Tears well in Ruby's eyes.

"There's no poison with Ruby's food. We all ate this morning at the boarding house," I say.

The bounty hunter picks up a biscuit and sniffs it. The sheriff steps away, allowing the doctor space to work.

"Who else was in your kitchen this morning?" The sheriff asks Ruby.

"Jo, Chord, and Mr. Weston," Ruby says. I give her shoulder a slight squeeze for support.

"We should find this, Weston," the deputy heads toward the door, stops, and asks, "What's he look like?"

"He's the gambler," I say. "I doubt he did this."

"I doubt it, too," The bounty hunter tosses a biscuit into his basket. Looking at Ruby, his face softens. "Did you stop anywhere or leave the basket unattended?"

Ruby pats my hand over her shoulder. "I came straight

here. I didn't want the food to get cold. When I got here, Ben — the sheriff was out, so I sat the basket on his desk with Mr. Payne."

"That's Deputy Payne," the other man says, his head tipped up and a finger pointing to his deputy star.

"When I got here, Payne was digging in the basket, and Conway asked if there was some for him," the sheriff says, stroking his chin in thought.

"I told him it was for the sheriff and to wait. He had no right going in the basket," Ruby says.

"Good thing I did. You could have killed one of us. I say we lock her up. Conway is as good as dead," Payne shouts.

"No one is dying," the doctor's voice comes from inside the cell. "Someone help me get this man down to my clinic."

"He can't go anywhere. He's a murderer," Payne says.

Sheriff Bentley holds up his hand. "I decide who goes where. Ruby, you can go back home. I'll return the basket later." The sheriff gives her a reassuring smile. "No one cooks like Ruby here. You're missing out if you're not staying at her boarding house."

"I'm all filled up," Ruby pulls back her shoulders.

"I bet you are." Payne saunters over by the desk. "Fine. Go. Sheriff and I will handle this." His gaze went to the bounty hunter.

Sheriff Bentley clears his throat. "Chord, you mind giving us a hand getting Conway over to the doctor's office?"

There goes our ride. I see it in the bounty hunter's eyes. "Jo, you take Ruby home, and I'll meet you back at the hotel after I help here."

"What about the horses?" I ask.

"I'll see to them you go on," he says.

"Is Mr. Conway going to be alright?" Ruby asks.

"It's food poisoning if I ever saw it," the doctor moves away from Conway. He's an older man with bushy white brows and a suit jacket worn to the threads. Doctoring doesn't pay much in Deadwood. Most folks spare a chicken or something from the garden, not having much gold or livestock this side of the gulch.

"Maybe you're right, Jo," Ruby says, resigned as we walk back to her place. "I should get some help running my place. What if my cooking kills Conway?"

What if, indeed? Conway can't die. He's my ticket to getting half of my land back and protecting Tail Feathers and the others in his tribe.

Conway dies, the bounty dies with him, and Coose's real killer will get away with the crime.

15

The prospect of getting on Lulu and heading out of town is too much to resist. My pony will have to stand tied to the rail for a while because Ruby needs me. I make her coffee, strong enough to put hair on a man's back. The kitchen is a mess, so she goes straight to washing the dishes. There are people in and out of the house. She doesn't pay them any mind. I go through the dining room, clearing what is left behind. Tucking my new gloves in my jacket, I hang it over a peg on the wall near the door.

Together, we get the chores done. By then, the hours have passed. Occasionally, Ruby looks out the window causing more wrinkles on her forehead. "Do you want to go to your room and get your Bible to pray before you have to prep for dinner tonight?"

A wistful smile comes to her face. She always told me praying takes a load off the soul. No matter how small, your problems are important to Jesus, as long as you remember to praise Him in the good times, too.

"Word gets out I killed Conway. No one's going to want to eat here. They'll all go back to the hotel," she says.

I push more coffee at her. One little incident has put a crack in her demeanor. Ruby survived her husband, losing a few barrens, and being a woman alone in the western frontier. Conway's poisoning is enough added pressure to have a woman on her knees.

Maybe I should join her. God knows why I need that bounty money. Conway needs to live.

"He's not dead," I assure her. He can't die. I need him.

Tail Feathers and his tribe are counting on me to protect them since my father is gone.

Too soon, the bounty hunter finds me. "Conway will live, but Ruby's banned from coming to the sheriff's office to see Bentley while he's got men in the hole."

"No hurt feelings." Ruby picks up the basin of dirty dishwasher to take outside and dump. "It's not a place I enjoy going. Benjamin knows where to find me if he wants to see me."

"Do you need help to get ready for dinner tonight?" I ask when Ruby steps back inside the kitchen.

"You two dining here tonight?"

I answer for both of us, "We're expected elsewhere."

The bounty hunter lifts a questioning brow. With my eyes, I hope he picks up on my cue.

"Eating at the hotel tonight again? Or Thompsons? You know you get dinner with your room."

"You should cut that to one meal a day. Save yourself some trouble and make a better profit," I remind her.

"Life isn't all about money," Ruby wages her finger. She's tired. The dark rings under her eyes prove it. I wish I could tell her to go to bed early, and I'll cook up some stew and biscuits to give her a break.

"We're headed out of town for the night," the bounty hunter goes over and grabs my jacket from the hook, holding it out for me. "Ready, wife?"

The way he says wife sends a prick under my nail like a burr. He says it to remind anyone within earshot that we're hitched.

"Off to the ranch we go." I slip on my jacket, pulling out my braid from underneath it.

"You take good care of her, you hear?" Ruby says to the bounty hunter.

"If anyone comes around and bothers you, let Bently know. I'll pass on an invitation to supper for him from you while we're gone."

She nods, and I wait until we're out of the house to ask. "You think someone is going to come around and harass Ruby?"

"Payne's got it in his head that she tried to kill Conway."

"Makes you wonder why? Is he trying to pin it on someone else to cover his own tracks?"

"It crossed my mind."

We're in front of my pony, Lulu. Her eyes are wide and alert. She dances to the side, pressing into the bounty hunter's roan stallion. She's not used to the people and the noises in town. Taking her reins, I try to reassure her. The bounty hunter mounts his horse and waits for me.

Figuring out how to work around this dress to mount is complicated. I yank up my petticoats, about to go astride as a bunch of men come out of the hotel. Harris and a bunch of Calvary uniforms hold up glasses in salute. Several of them shh the others and point my way. The bounty hunter reins his horse between us to block the view. Maybe I am showing a little too much leg?

"Swing your leg around the horn and sit sideways," the bounty hunter instructs. He reaches for Lulu's reins to keep her steady as she prances a little. My butt hits the saddle, and I almost go back when I feel a set of hands-on my backside.

"Steady there, darlin'. You wouldn't want to land back in the mud again, would you?"

Even the sound of the gambler's voice sets the bounty hunter on edge. He lets go of Lulu's reins, taking my arm to pull me his way as I balance in this sideways position. Once my leg bends around the horn, he yanks those petticoats down.

A whistle comes from the hotel, and men grin silly as they watch. The gambler's hands are still warming my behind.

"You can take your hands off my wife," the bounty hunter says.

"You're welcome," the gambler steps back and tips his hat in my direction. Those emerald eyes of his light up when he grins. Those dashing dimples of his send my belly flopping.

"Let's go, Jo," the bounty hunter sets out in a walk.

"Where are you heading?" the gambler asks.

Lulu follows without cue. All the time we were away, she must have been cozying up to the bounty hunter's stallion.

"To find Coose's killer." I wave, following behind the bounty hunter. The gambler gets up on the boardwalk out of the mud, jogging to keep up. "I'll come with you."

"Keep away from my wife," the bounty hunter says from ahead.

"Someone tried to kill Conway. One of us has to get to the bottom of this," the gambler's face flushes as he jogs beside me.

"Don't make me shoot," the bounty hunter warns.

"Then you'd best make sure nothing happens to him while we're gone." I nudge Lulu into a trot until we catch up with the bounty hunter. Once we're outside of town and in a place where the mud isn't so deep in the road, I pull up my petticoats, swing my leg down on the other side to better my balance, and we take off in a gallop.

The bounty hunter stays a good horse's length ahead. The roan stallion has longer legs than my pony. I'm also holding her back. There's no sense in showing off my legs, even if he's my husband.

A little while later, we slow back into a walk. The bounty hunter pulls his horse alongside mine. The stallion protests at slowing his stride for my painted pony.

My legs swinging at the side of my pony. If the bounty hunter notices, he keeps his gaze straight ahead.

"Your friends in the mountains teach you to ride?" he asks.

"I know how to do more things than you figure." Looking out at the wilderness ahead, my head tilts back, and I breathe. I don't care if it's damp with rain or chilled from the lack of sun. There's an unfamiliar smell outside of town. The further we ride away, the purer the air stirs around us.

"We should have waited to come out here," the bounty hunter keeps the stallion a distance away. "Whoever killed Coose is back in town. The deputy Bently hired will get chewed up and spit out before the month is out."

"He's not a swift one," I agree.

We follow the road for a long while before turning off to the west. There are cattle grazing in the distance and the afternoon sun continues to hide while the clouds spit on us.

My legs turn blue from the chilly rain drizzling over them. My stockings dampen, and I shiver the longer we ride.

Soon we come to where the large arch crosses the road, and smoke comes from a chimney in the distance.

"You best cover your legs up. We'll be coming into view of the ranch hands soon."

He rides ahead. Lulu speeds up to keep in stride with the stallion. I try to rein her to halt, but she trots on, justling me as I let one leg out of the stirrups. Grasping her mane, I swing the leg back around to bend over the horn. Lulu chooses the moment to shake her withers and her neck, almost dismounting me. "I don't like it either." I hold on.

Hooves approach behind me, spooking Lulu as she takes

off in a gallop. I hold tight and lean forward. The bounty hunter does a double take as we run past him.

He shouts at the riders. Lulu bucks, sending me over her neck. My rear end goes higher than my front end as I tumble down her neck and land on my feet.

Dazed, I hear someone say, "Now that's a neat trick. Can you teach me?"

My heart sticks in my throat. Gasping, I try to swallow it. A cowboy walks out of the barn. He's a dark skin man with a scar above his eye.

The bounty hunter halts beside Lulu. Dismounting, he asks, "You, okay? You're not hurt anywhere, are you?"

I don't answer. The man averts his gaze and goes back to the barn.

"Jo!" Ella Mae shouts from a bunkhouse several feet down. At first, she takes off in a walk, then a run.

"Ella Mae!" My legs give way. Thankfully, the bounty hunter has his arms around me. "Steady girl," he talks like I'm a horse.

I yank away.

"Show off!" She gives me the biggest hug. "Your father didn't teach you that," she says. "You've been holding out on me."

Glancing over at the bounty hunter, I shake my head. I'd forgotten all about Lulu. She stands, her head bouncing up and down. "She doesn't like the saddle."

"Lincoln and Buck are out checking on the west grazing land. All this rain is causing the creeks to swell. We lost some cattle the other day. They drowned trying to cross. Lincoln says cows aren't smart, but anyway, I'm so glad you're here. Erasmus should be in the barn. He'll see to the horses."

Ella Mae hooks her arm around mine. "Come on, I'll show you our place."

Pride fills her voice as she leads to one of the small bunkhouses.

"You don't live in the main house?"

Ella giggles, "Nope. Lincoln and I have our own place. His parents live in the main house, along with Amaryllis. Buck stays in the other bunkhouse with the hands. Since they're not married, their momma wouldn't let them stay together under the same roof."

"Your father didn't marry them?"

Ella Mae tenses. I should have known better than to mention her parents. "Your mother misses you," I say quietly. "She lent me one of your skirts and a pair of black heeled boots. I can see you get them back."

"Keep them," she brings me to the door. "This is our place, or it is until Lincoln builds us a house. He's picked the perfect place a few miles out."

Thinking of Ella Mae going further away doesn't sit right. Staying in town has softened me.

"We weren't expecting you, but there's an empty bunkhouse beside this one. A few of the hands ran off to join the railroad crew. It has left Buck and Lincoln at odds lately and old man Dawson, grumpier than a bear. Mrs. Dawson has been ill for the past few weeks. The doctor came out, but there is nothing he can do."

Listening to Ella Mae ramble about her new life makes me long for not a white picket fence but a home and a man, a girl, can call family.

Chitto, the one who gave me Lulu and another pony in order to buy me from my father in marriage, is the closest thing I've had to a family in the mountains. He and Tail Feather's tribe.

"It sounds like you're settling into becoming a rancher's wife. I take it Lincoln's parents weren't as bad as you thought?"

Ella Mae rolled her eyes. "They were thrilled to know he'd

married one of the reverend's daughters." Her voice whispers as she takes me inside her humble abode. "Unlike Buck. They're not at all happy with Amaryllis. Old man Dawson has her doing all the cooking for the hands, and she's not allowed out of the house past dark. If Buck wants to see her, he has to visit her at the house. She's been doing all the cleaning with Mrs. Dawson ill. I go over a few times a day to spend time with Mrs. Dawson and lend a hand while Lincoln and the others are away. Most of the time, I read the Good Book to her. She's got a lovely copy handed down from her family. One day, she said it'll go to Lincoln and me." Ella Mae tears up.

The small bunkhouse has a small potbellied stove, one bed, a washstand, a screen in the corner, and a small table over on the other side. A quilt hangs on the far wall, and another on the bed. The faded colors are warm, and Ella Mae heats coffee on the small stove. "The mercantile was out of tea before we left. Mrs. Dawson gave me permission to plant a garden once this rain lets us do anything."

Rubbing my arms, I feel a draft as Lincoln opens the door and sticks his head in to say hello.

"We've got company! Isn't that wonderful?" Ella Mae glows as she tells him.

I sit on one of the chairs, propping my elbow on the table, and resting my chin in my hand. Lincoln pulls Ella Mae close to him, whispering something in her ear. She gets a big grin on her face as she swats him away. "Go on then. We'll meet you at the house for supper."

Lincoln tips his hat to me, and then he's gone. I reach up, surprised my hat stayed on my head after the flip. I take it off and put it on the table. Finger by finger, I take off my gloves.

Ella Mae waits for the water to boil and adds the grains in the basket to percolate.

"I'm so glad you came," she says, her eyes reflecting the pain of her father's rejection.

"I wanted to see you. I was headed to check on you the night at the hotel, but then things went astray," I say.

She brushes down her skirt. "It spooked me. The sheriff spoke with us before we headed out here. 'The man's dead,' he said, and Mr. Conway from the railroad is the man I saw with the gun. He did it."

"I don't think so," and I fill her in on Conway, Daphne, and the bounty. I even go so far as to tell her about the new deputy, Conway's poisoning, and seeing Reed with Harris behind the stables.

"Who do you think did it?" Ella Mae gathers two cups for the coffee.

"Not Conway. At first, I thought Daphne."

"Mr. Coose offended her," Ella Mae points out.

"She thought Conway did it, and he thinks she did it, so he's trying to protect her."

Ella Mae's nose scrunches up in thought. "A man wouldn't do that unless it was family or his wife."

"Daphne said her father's got a suitor for her. She's so desperate she's chasing the gambler," I say.

Ella Mae pours the coffee. "Pfft. She wanted him weeks ago when she offered to smuggle you out of town to leave the gambler behind for her."

How long has Daphne known her father had a suitor for her?

"I found deeds in Reed's office. He's buying up land claims in the Black Hills."

"It's what banks do," Ella Mae blows on her hot coffee. "Sorry, I don't have any cream or sugar. We can get some from the main house if you want."

I wrap my hands around the metal cup, warming my chilled fingers. For May, the weather seems stuck in one temperature, chilly without a chance of sun to heat things up.

By the coziness of the bunkhouse, I doubt Ella Mae and Lincoln have had any troubles staying warm.

"It seems odd," Ella Mae tilts her head. "If Conway killed Coose, why would someone want to kill Conway?"

"That's a good point," Startled by the bounty hunter's voice, my coffee splashes over my hand. Hissing, I stick the red spot between my thumb and finger to suck on it. "You could knock," I mumble.

"Sorry ladies, Lincoln told me I could come on in."

"Do you want coffee?" Ella Mae asks, then frowns. "Oh, I've only got two cups."

"He can have mine," I slide it towards him, smiling in his direction. "It's black." Like the man in the barn. Scowling at my thoughts. The bounty hunter's eyes narrow as he reaches for the metal mug.

"I might have some sugar," Ella Mae fusses.

"Black is fine." the bounty hunter takes a sip, the steam rising from the rim.

Living in the mountains, you don't come across many people. The darkest skin tones have the misfortune of belonging to another. I'd heard from Chitto about them. Some came on the wagon trains headed to California. This is the first time I've seen one with my own eyes. People are fascinating creatures. Their motives for doing things baffle me, no matter their skin tone.

In Tail Feather's tribe, a man fought to prove his manhood. The women had a choice of the warriors. In this world, beyond the shelter of the Black Hills, the people have a different set of rules. Mulling it in my mind, I come back to Coose, Conway, Reed, and Daphne. Harris is in on it, I'm certain. What *it* is, I need to figure out.

"Ruby never left the basket. The only one who had his hands on it was Payne," I say.

"Who is Payne?" Ella Mae asks. Our discussions of suspects always perk her interest.

"Deputy Payne," I clarify.

"He new in town?" Ella Mae frowns.

"Sheriff took him right off the street. He rode into town wanting work, so the sheriff gave it to him."

I tap my lips, looking at Ella Mae, her eyes lighting up. I'm guessing we both have the same conclusion, so I voice it aloud. "He rode into town. I thought he came on the stage?"

"Me too, but Bentley said he found out later the kid came in on an old mule," the bounty hunter says.

"Kid? I thought you said this was a deputy. How old is he?" Ella Mae asks.

"About your age." I'm a few years older than Ella Mae. "Never mind the bounty hunter. He doesn't like the deputy, but the sheriff offered him the position first."

The bounty hunter slides the mug my way. He left me over half. "With good reason." Those eyes of his, dark from light stone to storm cloud grey. "I've got a wife to keep alive."

Ella Mae glances between us. Picking up her coffee, she sips, not saying another word. Tension curls around us as heady as the scent of coffee beans.

"We need to find out what Harris and Reed are really up to," I say, tearing my gaze away. "Ella Mae, do you remember seeing anything else at all? Something in the hall before you got to the open door?"

Ella stares out at the quilt behind me for a long moment. Her eyes meet mine again as she frowns. "Daphne Davenport rushed past. I think. It's all a blur. It's hard to say. I was so upset that night."

"I spoke to Daphne. Her father keeps her confined to the hotel to keep an eye on her. He and Harris have been trying to push things forward with the railroad. They offered the bounty hunter a job scouting."

"Jo," the bounty hunter warns.

"Ella Mae won't tell a soul," I assure him. "She knows more of my secrets than you do."

He crosses his arms. "Is that so?"

I bite my lip and duck my head. Ella Mae may know some of my secrets, but she doesn't know about Tail Feathers and Chitto.

"If I were trying to catch a murder and get the bounty," Ella Mae pipes in. "I'd look into the new deputy. You think the sheriff would have found about a person before putting a star on his chest?"

The bounty hunter leaves us without another word. Ella Mae chatters on about life on the ranch. She's so stuck on Lincoln that she didn't notice the change in the bounty hunter's posture when she mentioned the deputy's star.

She shows me the handkerchief she's working on for Lincoln, and we walk a bit despite the rain. There are dozens of chickens out back of the house, brown, black, and white striped ones dotting the yard. She points out where she'll plant a garden and where Lincoln will build her a house in the far distance.

I want what she has. One shouldn't covenant another's life. Nor do I envy her, and the divide shifted between her and her father. My chest aches for the family I won't ever have. I won't be my mother.

Who knows, maybe I won't be a wife for long either.

Once Coose's killer is found, and Conway is free, I'll have the rest of my land back. I will have to have a male relative by law handle it for me, and it makes me wonder who manages Ruby's house and property. I'll have to ask her after I find out more about Deputy Payne.

16

Saying goodbye to Ella Mae gets harder every time. I will see her for the May festival, she promised. She and Lincoln plan to return to town. Every time I bring up her mother, she changes the subject. Her eyes plead with me to let it go. Pearl couldn't say I didn't try. Ella Mae would have done the same for me.

We spend the entire night like two schoolgirls in Ella Mae's bed, talking and staying up until the lantern burns out. Lincoln must have bunked with the bounty hunter in the barn. While the mist dampens our faces the next day, a black cloud hovers over the bounty hunter. Several times I try to engage him in conversation. He grunts or the roan takes off in a gallop.

Riding back into town, more folk fill the streets with wagons and horses. In front of the saloon, two men take the boards covering the windows off. Polly's shrill voice cuts down the street. She holds an umbrella and wears a wool jacket.

Lulu halts as I watch across the street. "What is Polly doing badgering those men at the saloon?"

The bounty hunter nudges his horse to keep going. Without a cue, Lulu rears as a board clamors down. A man shouts, and she jumps sideways. My rear slides back off the saddle. With my leg hooked around the horn to keep my legs covered, I fall short of hitting the street. Lulu takes off with me hanging upside down against her. Pulling on the reins turns her head, but she guns it for the stables. My heart and lungs are screaming as I can't muster a sound. Dangling at Lulu's side, the pony shoots inside, where Hank grabs hold of her under the bridle.

The bounty hunter jumps down from his horse behind me. Two arms go beneath me as Hank untangles my leg on the other side. I hate saddles! Biting my lip, I don't let the humiliation or pain show.

Why is it that I suddenly feel Lulu has it in for me?

"Next time we go out, we're taking a wagon," the bounty hunter says.

The reassurance there will be a next time tickles me in all the right places. Back on my feet, he doesn't let me lean on him for too long. "You good?"

"Right as rain."

"I'll help Hank with the horses. You think you can make it back to the hotel without getting yourself in any more trouble?" He's mad, but I don't know what I did.

Brushing down my skirts and straightening my jacket, I reach up, and my hat is gone. Panic swells in my chest. I spin around in circles. "My hat!"

The bounty hunter shoves it my way. "You're lucky you didn't get trampled," he practically growls.

"Whose idea was it to make me ride sideways on a saddle in town? Lulu never had a saddle on her before yesterday. She's a mountain horse, not a city mare."

His head tips back. Grabbing my hat, I stalk around Lulu. Taking a second, I give her a hug around her neck and whisper, "I forgive you."

Hank steps out of my way, and I burst out of the stables.

Lord, don't let me feel this tomorrow.

Marching down the street, I encounter Polly. "Why don't you leave these men alone?"

She laughs. "These men are helping me open the saloon back up." She gets a giant grin on those painted lips. "That's right, honey buns, you're looking at the new owner of the Deadwood Saloon. Soon folk around here will call it Polly's Place." She pats me on the shoulder. "Don't you worry none. My door is always open to that husband of yours." She winks.

Balling my hands into a fist around my hat, I'm about to push past her when an awful thought strikes me.

"You weren't faithful to my father, were you?"

Polly's grin disappears. "Your father didn't deserve to have a faithful wife. He treated me like a slave, kept me trapped on the mountain."

"Not. What. I. Asked."

Her hands plant on her hips. The men behind me pry off the boards. My teeth clench with each sound of a hammer pulling on the nails. Glen, the old owner, tried to drug me and kill me in this very saloon.

"If you haven't noticed, honey buns, there are more men than women out here. Send him Momma's way when you can't handle that bounty hunter of yours. I'll take care of him."

Her smug expression wipes off quickly as my fist connects with her nose. No one can ever say I hit like a girl. The bounty hunter taught me to tuck in my thumb, but it didn't make it hurt any less.

How quickly you forget the pain of your knuckles hitting flesh.

Polly howls and crumbles to the ground. Blood seeps between her fingers. The two men on the ladders come down quick. One hauls me off to see the sheriff, while the other takes Polly to see the doctor.

Sheriff Bentley shakes his head at me. "You punched Polly Dean? Isn't she your mother?"

"She had it coming." I shake out my fist, trying to ease the smartness tingling between my fingers. Once again, I let my temper get the best of me.

"I saw it, Sheriff. Hauled off and punched poor Mrs. Dean for no reason."

"Poor Mrs. Dean," I scoff. "She's trying to steal my land and my husband. She insulted me, sheriff. A woman has a right to defend her honor."

"Sheriff," Robbie's voice calls up the street. "You better come quick. There is trouble at the bathhouse."

"If it isn't one thing, it's another." Sheriff Bentley tosses up his arms.

"What you going to do, Sheriff?"

Indecision fills him as Polly hobbles into the doorway. "Arrest her, Sheriff," she huffs, big fat tears rolling down her cheeks.

"Come now, Mrs. Dean, let's have a look at your nose." I recognize the doctor behind her.

"Is Conway going to be alright?" I call to him.

"I want to press charges," Polly calls out as the white-haired doctor tugs her out of the sheriff's office.

"Sheriff!" Robbie calls.

"Where's Payne?" the sheriff thunders.

Robbie shrugs.

The sheriff runs his hand through his hair. "Fine. Dean, get yourself into a cell. I'll deal with you later."

The man holding me doesn't even need to wrestle with me. He shoves me into a cell, and the sheriff locks me in. Shaking his head, he heads out.

"You going to leave her here alone?" the man asks.

"Out. I've got other problems to deal with."

Everyone glances over to Conway's cell. He moans, his back to the rest of us. Lucky to be alive, I don't think he'll be much company while I'm here.

The sheriff makes everyone leave. He closes the door, and I hear the lock. Taking a seat on the small cot, I lean back against the wall and wait for the deputy to come.

"You can't stay out of trouble, can you?" the bounty hunter fumes, pacing in front of my cell. Conway moans in his sleep from the next cell over. The doctor said it would take a few days for the man to get well from the poisoning.

"If I'd have known you would go around punching people, I wouldn't have taught you to make a fist," the bounty hunter says.

"She had it coming."

He grips the bars, his gaze locks on mine, deadly as the six-shooter he carries. "What makes a woman clock another in the nose?"

"She insulted me," I say, almost amused by his behavior. Nevertheless, a small part of me is happy I'm safe on this side of the bars.

"What possible could she have said?" he asks.

"It was about you."

His shoulders lower, but the anger continues to brew in his eyes. "What about me?"

"She'll be more than happy to entertain you in her bedroom at the saloon anytime," I inform him, looking away.

"Most women have catfights."

"I am not most women." I pick at a piece of lint on my jacket.

He leans his forehead against the bars. "Come here, Dimples."

I shake my head.

"I should have known you were trouble from the start," he says.

Standing up, I keep a few feet away from the bars. "I guess you wished you didn't marry me." It's as good of a time as any to admit the truth. "You must have been desperate to secure your ten percent of my claim."

When my father got shot, I made a deal with the bounty hunter. I needed his help, so I offered him ten percent of my mine claim in the mountains.

"I got enough money of my own, Dimples. I don't need yours," and he's sincere in saying it.

My heart skips a beat. I move a little closer to the bars. "Then why did you marry me? You could have left me to the gambler and moved on to your next bounty."

"I don't like seeing women taken advantage of, Jo. I can't protect you if you keep causing trouble."

"I can take care of myself."

Behind us, the door opens and closes. The bounty hunter moves to block the view into my cell. "How's that going for you?"

I wrap my arms tight around myself. Having been here a few hours, I realize I should have thought this through more. "I don't enjoy being in a cage." A small cage, at that, but I try not to let my fear show on my face.

"I can talk the sheriff into letting you out before morning. Usually, a brawl will land you in a cell for a day or two. This wasn't much of a brawl, was it?"

"No," I say.

His eyebrow quirks up. The anger slowly fades from him.

I step closer, seeing someone take a seat at the desk. "You can't get me out of here yet."

His hand reaches in, grabs my arm, and hauls me closer to the bars. "What are you up to?" his voice lowers.

My hand goes over his around the bars. To anyone looking, we're having an intimate moment.

"Don't you see? If I'm here, then I can keep an eye on Payne. I might even get him to talk."

Surprise registers in those stone-cold eyes. "What crazy person put that idea in your head? Ella Mae? I shouldn't have taken you out there."

"No. It was mine. Don't blame her." I plea in a soft whisper.

He searches my face, his expression grim. "I don't like this."

"She crushed my father when she left. He carried her picture in the bottom of his boot so he could step on her face every day. Now I know why. All this time, I thought it was something I did. Something Earl did. But she left because she's... she's a...."

"Dimples," the bounty hunter groans. "Violence isn't the answer. It'll come back on you two-fold."

"Says the man who hunts down the bad guys and kills them for a living."

"I only kill when they're about to kill me."

I see it in his eyes, a deep, haunting torment.

I resign. "I won't do it again."

My hand isn't healed from the last time I used my fist. One of the parts of my body that might not have ached tomorrow, and here I go, a glutton for punishment.

"You barely survived a few minutes in Ruby's pantry."

"There is light here."

"Until it gets dark, and you don't know who Bently or Payne will toss in here tonight. Polly's opening the saloon, then every shady cowboy from here to Silver Valley will ride back into town to wet their whistle. This isn't any place for —"

I finish for him, "A woman. I know. Give me enough time to see what I can glean from Payne, then you can take me and lock me away in our hotel room for the night."

He presses his lips together in thought. "You've got before

supper. I'm not taking any chances with the food, and it will get dark in here. I don't like this."

"I need the bounty money. Please, Chord."

"You'll call me Chord from here on out."

"Anything you want."

"I'll be back before supper. At least I'll know where you are while I take care of some business of my own."

I'm about to ask him what kind of business when Payne raps his knuckles on the desk. "Times up, lovebirds."

The bounty hunter runs a finger down my nose and presses to my lips. "Behave."

Payne slinks back behind the sheriff's desk as the bounty hunter leaves.

"There's no time limit for visitors," I say.

"There is if I say there is." Payne takes a seat, leans back, and puts his feet up. "Now be a quiet prisoner. It's been a long day, and it will be an even longer night. I need some shuteye."

"Some deputy you are," I huff, settling back down on the cot.

"Some kind of woman, you are getting locked up. There's one kind I can think of," he tosses right back at me. His lude grin doesn't scare me.

"Touch me, and my husband will track you down, deputy or not."

Payne pulls out his gun and lays it on the desk. His hand trembles slightly. "You're not the first woman he's gunned down men over. Keep it up, Mrs. Townes, and you'll have your husband trading places with you."

"How do you know what the bounty hunter has done?" Chiding myself, I repeat his name over and over in my head. *Chord. Chord. Chord.*

Payne gets up and comes closer to my cell. "There aren't very many people who know. The man was once the best tracker of all the Texas Rangers, then he snapped and disappeared for many years. Guess we know where he's been all this time."

Payne goes back to his desk, feet up, hat covering his face. The conversation is over. I curl up on the cot, mulling over what he said. Several times I try to engage him in conversation. Payne ignores me.

A half an hour later, the door of the sheriff's office opens, and I fear the bounty hunter has returned for me early.

"Lem," the man says, pushing Payne's feet off the desk. He's a short man, wearing a grey Calvary coat. His hair extends to his shoulders, and a beard covers half his face. I thought the Calvary made their men stay clean and respectable.

His eyes glance my way, and I stay down, keeping my eye half hooded to foreign sleep.

Payne yawns, stretching. He stills. "Brody? You crazy?" Payne hisses, "I told you not to come back here!"

Both men glance over at me.

"What is with the woman?" the one called Brody asks. "Looks too proper for a nightingale."

"Catfight. Punched the saloon matron and broker her nose," Payne steps in front of my view. "She's Townes wife."

"Ranger Townes?"

"Told you he's a bounty hunter now."

"He hasn't left yet?" Brody asks.

"He got a new wife. Seems he is sticking around for now." Brody grunts.

"The sheriff will be back soon to let her out. Townes won't stand to let his wife in jail for the night. You can't be here when he does."

"I'm not worried about the sheriff." Brody shoves Payne back a step. "I gave you one job to do."

Payne's body tenses. "I'm working on it. You think this job is easy?"

"Try harder. You mess this up, and I'll kill you." The man named Brody leans to look in my direction. I don't dare move.

Payne looks over his shoulder, keeping his voice low. "I'll get it done. Now go."

Brody leaves while Payne makes his way back closer to my cell. My heart hammers as he stares at me for a good long while. There is no chance I'll be having any more words with him. It takes all my effort to keep my breathing steady and pretend I'm sleeping.

"Shame you're going to end up dead," he says. I pant through my mouth, knowing that he'll notice if I hold my breath.

The sheriff returns not a moment too soon. Payne turns away to talk to him. All I want is to jump up and ask him to let me out to get away and find the bounty hunter.

Allowing my eyes to flutter shut to keep up the rouse, it's been a long two days of riding and staying up late with Ella Mae.

Chord is in my cell when my eyes open again, his hand on my arm gently shaking me awake.

Behind him, Payne stands, keys in hand, swinging them around his fingers. The deputy looks down his nose at me.

Sitting up, I rub my eyes. My body hurts all over, and I'm not sure if it's the cot or Lulu's back-breaking stunt catching up with my muscles.

The bounty hunter holds out his hand for me. I keep my eyes on Payne as the bounty hunter pulls me to my feet.

Next to me, the sound of the railroad owner snores resumes. Earlier I heard him wrenching and almost wanted to do the same. I say another prayer for him. I need him alive, but also, I've seen the suffering of those in Tail Feather's tribe go through sickness. Someone wanted Conway dead, and they tried to use Ruby. Why?

A groan escapes my lips, and I bite it down as the bounty

hunter yanks me to my feet. "No dinner for you tonight, wife. It's straight to bed."

Payne chuckles behind us.

Outside the sheriff's office, I tell the bounty hunter all about the man named Brody. One eye closed, the side of his jaw tightened, I ask, "Do you know him?"

"Brody Brownell," the bounty hunter grits his teeth. The war goes on in his face. "He's wanted."

"This is good." It might not be enough to connect Payne to poisoning Conway, but they're planning something, or perhaps Payne needs to finish the job. If Brody's a wanted man, we can also capture him, and I can pay my own way again.

Ella Mae may be on to something. The May festival is coming up soon.

"No, Jo. We find who killed Coose and pay off the gambler. Brody, or any members of the Brownell gang, are no concern of yours."

17

True to his word, the bounty hunter walks me to my room at the hotel. There is no way I'm going to stay here while he tracks the killer without me. You would think by now he'd know better than to try and keep me from getting the bounty.

The worst thing he could have said to me was for me to leave Brody Brownell and the bounty hunting to him.

Well, I'll show him. I'll find Coose's killer before him. I'll prove I'm not the trouble he thinks I am.

Counting to a hundred is as far as I can get until my patience runs out. My hat goes on the bed, followed by my gloves and coat. First, I freshen up. The ripe odor of the jail cell will haunt me for a long time.

Unbraiding my hair, I brush through it with my fingers. Leaving it down, I grab the handle to find it won't budge. Rattling the door, I slap my hand against it.

Out of one jail cell into another, my chest heaves. Rushing over to the window, I throw back the curtains. The window won't budge. Searching around the frame, I look for an extra lock I might have missed. My finger graces over the top of a nail. He nailed the window frame shut.

Fury burst through me. Picking up the nearest thing, my hat flies across the room, tapping the door and landing with a soft thud.

Curling my fists, I turn to the window, smashing my fist against the window frame, the wood sending splintering pain through my fingers. Crying out, I sink to the floor. I couldn't even hit the right target. I missed the glass.

I missed everything.

Down on the floor in a mess of skirt, boots, and tears, I nurse my hand. Me and my stupid temper. When will I learn?

Closing my eyes, I tilt my head back against the wall. Where is Ella Mae when I need her? Or Chitto?

Outside the window in the distance, the mountains mock me.

At some point, I fell asleep because the sound of banging on my door roused me. My hand and my head pound. Grungily, I get to my feet. The banging continues. "Stop. I'm coming." Staggering, I grab the door and hiss at the pain in my hand. One of these days, I'll learn to take my frustration out in a different way.

The door swings open, and Minnie from the Swanson Sisters Bathhouse stands before me. In her arms lies a neatly folded stack of clothes. "Chord thought you'd like to change and freshen up after the past few days. I came last night, but you didn't answer. You must have been exhausted, and rightly so." Minnie waltzes right into my room. Her black hair is pulled back in a smooth bun, and her hazel eyes gleam with amusement.

"I guess I don't have to ask where my husband's been," I mutter, shutting the door.

"You can put the clothes down. I can wash up and change on my own." My arms wrap around the uncomfortable corset. A few weeks ago, in the bathhouse, Minnie did my hair. She's also the same woman I caught the bounty hunter with when I sought him out at the bathhouse. While I caught him with his shirt off, I've forgiven him and moved on. It's not like our marriage is real, but it let me see a side of him I hadn't expected.

"I have no doubt you can, Mrs. Townes, but your husband sent me here specifically to help you get you ready for the day. Have you seen your hair?" Minnie "Tsks." She doesn't belong over at the bathhouse. Minnie came here as a mail-order bride and became a widow a couple of days later.

Reaching up, I touch the tangled mess. "My hair should be the least of his worries." I hold on to my throbbing hand, my eyes scratchy from crying. "I suppose you helped him get dressed this morning, too, before he sent you over?"

Minnie puts down the clothes on the bed. The gold brocade coverlet remains without a wrinkle. "Chord is an honorable man. He helped me."

"I know, he told me."

Minnie smooths down her skirts. She wears a dark-colored dress with an apron over it. "Then there shouldn't be a problem."

"It seems the bounty hunter has a weakness for damsels in distress."

"Ah, but you are the first one he married." Minnie put her hands on her hips.

"I'm not his first wife," but if she's seen my bounty hunter's scars, she knows about his first wife. Chewing my lip, I can't decide whether I should ask her. A deal is a deal, and I shouldn't go poking in his business. But a woman should know things about her husband.

"I haven't got all morning. Sit, and we'll tackle your hair first."

"I don't have a brush," I say.

"Sit, I've got one." Minnie pulls one out from her skirt pocket. "You hurt your hand. Again."

"The bounty hunter told you." A pang of jealously radiates in my chest.

"Don't take it personally." She gestures, and I take a seat in the chair on the far wall. "Chord said you were impulsive and temperamental. He supposed it came from living up in the wilderness. After meeting you, the way you boldly came in to bathe at the sisters' house, I told him more women should be brave as you."

"I tipped over the entire tub of water at Ruby's place, which is why we have to stay here."

She laughs. "Maybe it's better you come over to the bath-house. It's better to come in the middle of the day. You don't have to worry about as many comings and goings," she says, standing behind me.

An hour later, my wild tresses are smoothed, braided, and twisted at the back of my head. "You've got a real talent," I tell her. "You don't belong in the sister's bathhouse anymore as I belong in this hotel," I confess.

"It's not what you think. I clean and cook and help the sisters. It is not so bad." The wan smile on her face tells me she's sugar-coating it.

I slip on the skirt to find it splits. This is what Grace and the bounty hunter meant by a riding skirt. It's a pair of wide-leg pants with another layer over it, appearing like a skirt. The blouse is green. I'm detecting a theme in my attire. At least my ribs aren't confined, and the sisters are comfortable. I can live with these new dudes. As a matter of fact, I think they are now officially my new favorite duds.

"If you ever decide, you don't want to stay there," I tell her as we leave my room. "Ruby may be in some need of help."

We're halfway down the hall when I realize I forgot my hat. "Didn't you wear a bonnet?"

"It stopped raining last night."

"I don't go anywhere without mine." You never know when you'll get caught with the sun in your face.

I turn around. On the way back, shouting comes from inside one of the rooms across from mine. Curiosity lassoing me towards the door, I hear a crash, a shout, and a startle as the door yanks open.

Jumping back, Mr. Davenport burst out of the hallway. Seeing me brings him to an abrupt halt. Behind him, red-faced Harris glares at me one moment, then slams the door shut the next.

"What are you doing here?" Davenport blusters.

"I was on my way to breakfast." I try not to let his stout frame intimidate me.

"This close to a man's door?" He reaches up to smooth out his hair.

"I thought I would ask Daphne to join me."

"I believe my daughter is still asleep in her room. A woman of her breeding needs her beauty sleep." Then he sweeps his gaze down over me and back to my face. "Some more than others."

I squeeze my hand into a fist. The ache holds my ire in place along with the pains from yesterday.

"Have a nice morning," I mutter as he passes me. Heading for my room, I decide my hat isn't as important. Turning around, I spy Harris softly, closing the door and heading down the hall opposite the stairs.

He's ahead of me, so I wait a breath, then walk after him. My heart picks up speed. Harris walks like a man on a mission.

He glances over his shoulder, scowling at me. Giving him a wobbly smile, I turn towards a door and lift my hand to knock. The door beside this one opens, and I hear, "Jo-Dee! What are you doing? That's my father's room."

"Oh," I think, quick to cover for my blunder. "I got mistaken. I thought it was yours."

Daphne blocks my view as she comes out into the hallway. She's got on a navy gown with a matching jacket. "You were coming to check on me again?" Her hand touches her heart.

"I'm headed to Ruby's for breakfast. Would you like to come along for tea?" Eventually, I would have to do something about my penniless state.

"I'd be delighted. However, I have a stop to make on our way, if you don't mind." She walks beside me. "Two. We have to stop down in the kitchen first. Mr. Warner promised he would put together a little something for me."

I bet he did, but I keep that tidbit to myself. Down the hall, Harris has disappeared.

"You're up early," I say. "Your father said you like to sleep in."

"It's hard to get any shut-eye around here with the shouting. My father and Mr. Harris don't seem to agree on things. They should ask Thomas, but it's like they both have him written off." She pauses at the top of the stairs. "You look good, by the way. The dark brown skirt suits you. I suppose I'll be the one having to adapt to this harsher living than going back home."

In her way, I think Daphne gave me a compliment. I don't let it go to my head. Me and Daphne are not friends or in the sense of anything deeper than an acquaintanceship.

"You intend to stay?" I ask.

"I heard my father talking to the bank gentleman about renting a house here in town. Warner refused to offer my father a monthly rate. Daddy said he wasn't staying at the boarding house," Daphne sniffs.

Way to go, Warner. For a man who wants to court the lady and lose his guests, he's not acting smart about it.

Daphne takes the stairs, her hand gliding elegantly on the banister. Try as I may, I don't possess the gracefulness she does.

Sherman looks up from his papers long enough to direct

Daphne to the dining room. Warner has his sleeves rolled up. Hardly anyone sits in the dining room this time of the morning. He has a table for two with tea ready.

Daphne and I partake of the offered setting. Warner brings biscuits and jam. He frowns my way, but he's too polite to point out I'm sitting in his chair.

"Has your father mentioned anything more about a suitor?" I say purposely in front of Warner. He stalls behind Daphne, making work of rolling down his sleeves.

"No. He and Mr. Harris are too busy shouting at the bank man some days. My father is under pressure with the workers coming into town to build the station and the other ones in the mountains. They've got men out cutting down lumber to build more houses and expand the town. My father doesn't think we should build many houses. The men have been living in tents as they move along. Mr. Harris and Mr. Reed seem to think the additional houses provided from the railroad will bring in more income for the town." Daphne spreads jam over her biscuit. What I could really go for are some of Ruby's eggs and bacon. She's going to need another flock of chickens if Deadwood keeps bringing in more people. I can't see them staying, so I stuff my mouth with a biscuit and keep those thoughts to myself.

"Your father is an investor, right?"

Daphne nods, sipping her tea.

Warner lingers nearby, and she lifts her head to speak with him. "Would you mind getting that delivery we discussed? I would so ever be grateful." She bats her lashes, and Warner takes off.

A woman who can command a man with the flick of a lash is more dangerous than a man with a gun if you ask me. Someday I'll have to ask her how she does it.

With Warner gone, Daphne takes the last biscuit. She spreads jam over it, then wraps it in a cloth napkin, slipping it into her pouch on her lap as she says, "My father thinks I'm dumb, but I know I'm the most valuable asset he has. Without me and my money, he's got nothing left to invest."

Sounds familiar. Without me and my land, the gambler has nothing to barter with the railroad.

Maybe Daphne and her father are worse off than I thought.

Warner returns with a small basket. Daphne lets him know how much she appreciates him going through the trouble. She knows how to coat it on thick with compliments. Warner's goofy grin as we leave tells me Daphne knows what she's doing.

I wait until we're down the street outside the hotel before asking, "Where are we headed?"

"Over to the sheriff's office. I'm glad you're coming with me this time. The deputy makes me uncomfortable. The man has lude eyes. He doesn't give me a moment alone to speak with Thomas. The doctor said he was lucky to have had a mild case."

My stomach gurgles, remembering when Glen tried to poison me with fake whiskey. He told me it was tea and forgot to add the part where he laced it with laudanum.

Inside the sheriff's office, the deputy sits at the desk. "Back so soon?" he chuckles.

Daphne tilts up her chin, not realizing his words were directed at me. "I've come to visit Mr. Conway."

He stands up behind the desk. "What you got there?"

Primly she sets the basket on the desk. "I had the hotel make up a basket as a practice run for the festival. After Mr. Conway's food incident, I want to make sure he has something safe to eat."

"I'll have to go through this, you understand?" Deputy Payne looks at us suspiciously.

"By all means." She opens the basket, plucking out a wrapped cloth. She opens it to reveal a few stripes of bacon.

My mouth waters seeing them. "While you inspect the food and help yourself to a few samples, I'll visit with Mr. Conway for a few minutes."

"And you?" Deputy Payne looks at me.

"I'm with her," I say.

Deputy Payne occupies himself with the basket. The scents of bacon, eggs, and freshly baked bread wafer from the basket.

I keep close to Daphne as she approaches Mr. Conway. "Thomas," she says.

Mr. Conway gets up from his cot. "You shouldn't keep coming here," he says.

"I needed to ensure they are treating your right. I'm scared." Her eyes fill with tears, and her chin wobbles. "I know you didn't do it."

He reaches between the bars, sliding his hand against her cheek. It's such an intimate gesture. I don't know what to make of it. My father never laid a kind hand on me, nor do I have experience with male family members. I'm certain the way Conway gazes at Daphne, there is more here than her father's business partner friendship.

"Have you found the killer?" Conway asks.

"I can't say," and I can't. I've narrowed it down to Payne and Brody Brownell, but I'll have to prove they're in it together. The crucial element missing is why?

Conway slips his hand from Daphne's cheek. "You've only got a few days. The rain has let up, and the stage is coming in a few days. The sheriff says a judge will be on it."

Daphne keens low in her voice. "You didn't do it." She reaches in her purse, pulls out the covered biscuit, and slips it into Conway's hand.

His handshakes, but he smiles and tucks it in his pants pocket. His eyes find mine, and my insides go cold.

"If you have come to ask more questions or ensure our deal is good, I had already reassured the bounty hunter when he visited me last evening. I have told him all I know, and I keep my word."

Watching while the two whisper, I listen to their conversation. Conway keeps reassuring her, but I can tell there is weariness in his expression. Soon Daphne and I head out of the sheriff's office. By the time we go, Payne has sampled half the basket. I hope Daphne didn't try to poison him.

Outside, by the wanted posters tacked to the side of the wall, I stop to take a gander. There. In the top left corner, the man I saw with the deputy stares back at me in black and white. He's different from the picture, but the eyes and the crooked teeth are the same. He grew a beard, but I identify the man beneath.

"Are we going to the boarding house? Do you know if Mr. Weston still stays in one of the rooms?"

"I'm not sneaking you into his room," I say.

Daphne gasps, covering her mouth with her gloved hand. "Why, Jo-Dee, how could you think like that?"

I give her a look. Proper lady or not, getting caught with the bounty hunter tying my corset strings got us hitched, and I don't dare put that idea in Daphne's head about the gambler. Of all the men, why can't she choose Warner? Reed? Anyone else?

"Is Mr. Conway the suitor your father, chose for you?" I ask.

Daphne stays under the roof of the cafe. It's not raining anymore, but the clouds have a way of deceiving you into thinking it will be a dry, sunny day. The sooner things dry up, the sooner I can return to my room at Ruby's.

"No." She whispers, her hands clasped together, "but Thomas agrees with my father on the arrangement."

"Is that why you tried to poison him and kill him?"

"Kill him?" The look of horror on her face guts me. "I told

you I didn't do it. You've been trying to pin it on me all this time."

"The last thing Mr. Conway ate before getting poisoned was a biscuit. I saw it lying beside him. Ruby makes her biscuits light and fluffy they can float. The ones from the hotel are denser and dry, which is why they take a lot of jam to swallow. I watched you give the hotel biscuit you put in your purse to Mr. Conway."

"Wouldn't that make Mr. Warner or one of his staff the killer? The biscuits came from the hotel kitchen." Daphne's lavender eyes darken.

"You could have tampered with it before giving it to him." I am probably wrong and grasping at straws with time running out.

Daphne pulls back her shoulders, her chin tilted. "If you must know, Thomas often indulged me on the train. We have tea and biscuits because no one on the train could prepare the pastries right. It felt fitting when I visited him to take him a biscuit. Those interactions are dear to me. Thomas doesn't treat me like an inept female. He listens, and we have intelligent conversations. I would never harm him, and the fact you would continue to accuse me of murder is insulting."

"I'm trying to help Mr. Conway."

"You almost had me fooled. Pretending you wanted to be more of a lady. Get yourself all dressed up and do your hair. Fanning over Mr. Weston when you're married to the bounty hunter. You're no lady. I heard all about your mother, taking over the saloon, and living at the bathhouse. It's no wonder you're chasing after Mr. Weston. Like mother, like daughter. We can all pray Mr. Townes comes to his sense and has the judge annual your marriage for his sake. Even a man like him would have shame of his wife behaving as you do."

Every word she says strikes me like a blow. One deeper than the last. Curling my fists, I clutch the hem of my jacket, and my knuckles whiten. My hand aches, but if I lash out, I'll prove her point.

"I'm nothing like my mother," I say, my throat closing.

Behind me, a trail of ladies passes us, heading inside the cafe. "Daphne, you must join us," Hannah Baker calls. "Sorry, Mrs. Townes, this meeting is for the single ladies in town."

All three of them, four counting Daphne, but I hold my tongue. There is a reason some women don't marry as soon as others. I think of Minnie and Ruby, both widowed. I think of Daphne, who has a suitor and chases another. Chitto offered to marry me when I was sixteen summers old.

"You, Jo-Dee, are not my friend," Daphne informs me. "Don't try coming around me again." She marches into the cafe', where Hannah Baker, Lottie Larson, and several ladies have gathered inside. I reach up and pat the braids twisted in the back of my head.

"I'm not my mother," I say to the glass, looking in the cafe. Standing here won't catch the killer or get me the bounty.

18

Doctor Chierhart lives on a side street in Deadwood. His office is a side room in his house, and he rarely keeps a patient anywhere else. By the looks of the building, it's one of the newer ones built since Deadwood came into existence. Maybe this doctoring thing isn't as bad as I thought.

Stepping up to his porch, I'm pleasantly surprised by the herbs growing on the other side of the window. An older woman opens the door. "May I help you?"

"Is the doctor in?"

Her eyes are kind, and her lips thin for a moment. "He's gone on a call out to one of the ranches."

Panic sets in as my first thoughts go to Ella Mae. She's the bestest friend I've got. "Do you know which one?"

"I can't say," the woman invites me inside and out of the day's chill. The clouds have held their own, and not a drop of rain has fallen. "Are you hurt? Do you need help for someone else?"

I think of my hand and all the bumps and bruises from Lulu, but I shake my head. It's my fault, and they'll heal in a few days. "I was hoping to ask him a question. Maybe you can help me."

"If it's a womanly thing, my husband prefers to refer the gals to me. Why don't we sit down? Are you married?"

She's too kind to deny. "Yes. Recently, actually."

"You've not a mother or a sister?" We step into a cozy little sitting room where the fire warms the room enough to ward off the spring chill from outside. Dried flowers rest on the mantle along with several ornate vases. Hanging above the fireplace is a tomahawk with feathers. She notices me staring at it.

"Irvine, Dr. Chierhart, got that while serving with his regiment. I've always found it grizzly, but he likes it there. I suppose he earned it, helping to clear the path for us to make way into the territory."

Swallowing hard, I turn away. I'm not here to argue over politics. What's been done is done, and I can't change the past. If I could, I would have stopped Earl from coming down off the mountain and starting the chain of events that led me here. Ella Mae would tell me it would happen, anyway. Who are we to change the plans God has for us? Fighting it makes it worse.

"Are you feeling well?"

Perhaps seeing the tomahawk has me looking a little green around the gills. "Fine."

"How long has it been?"

When I don't answer, she pats me on the shoulder. "It's easy to lose track in the honeymoon phase. You'll want to count and pay attention. It's natural for things to happen in the occurrence of marriage."

It's then I understand. My neck gets hot, spreading up to the tip of my ears. "Oh no. That's not why I'm here."

I learned all about the birds and the bees when I came of age. Chitto's mother took it on herself, seeing as Chitto chose me for a wife. Although I ended up with the ponies, Chitto had to go back to his tribe empty-handed.

"If it's not that, then what is the problem?" The doctor's poor wife looks at me, confused.

"It's about Mr. Conway. The doctor helped him. He was poisoned. I was hoping he could tell me what poisoned him."

"Mr. Conway? The railroad man?" she asks.

"The one. He hired me to clear his name, and I'm trying to figure out who and how would try to harm him."

Her gentle smile turns upside down. "Didn't you say you're married?"

"To a bounty hunter. We're partners." It's sort of true. I got his name, and he's getting a portion of my claim rights.

"Irvine told the sheriff when he called on Mr. Conway in his jail cell. He's a quiet man, a bit more polished for these parts than we're used to having around."

"Sounds like him. He was lucky we discovered he was ill from the poison when we did, and the doctor came," I say.

She waves her hand. "You've got it all wrong. Mr. Conway wasn't poisoned. Well, he was, but not intentionally. He got sick because the food he ate was spoiled. Irvine stopped by the boarding house before he headed out to the ranch. There is no telling how many people ate the food."

"At the boarding house?"

She nodded. "I was going to head over there and see if I could be of any help."

I shook my head. "Are you sure it was Ruby's place?"

She shrugged, "Mr. Conway said the last food he ate came from there. The sheriff wasn't looking too hot either when Irvine gave him the news."

"Food poisoning," I say, pressing my hand to my stomach.

"Are you and your husband staying at the boarding house?" she asks, keeping her hand on my arm.

"No. We've been at the hotel for the past few days." But that's not what has my stomach rolling. "Thank you for letting me know. I should go check on my husband. We were thinking of taking a room there."

"Keep hydrated, dear. Irvine said that it's not contagious unless you ate the bad food."

Let's hope not. I thank the doctor's wife.

"If you have questions, I'm always here."

My aching hand forgotten, I walk, okay, run. Once I'm back on Main Street, I stick to the boardwalk to keep from getting my boots stuck in the mud.

"Where are you going, honey?" Polly calls after me, standing outside the saloon. "Don't stop and say hi to your momma or anything. You know where I am when you're ready to negotiate."

Her voice fades, and everything else becomes a blur. Approaching Ruby's front door, a sign hangs from the knob. 'Closed. No Vacancy.'

Since Ruby keeps the door unlocked during the day for boarders to come and go, I help myself inside. The place is quiet. "Ruby?"

Closing the door, I find the parlor empty. The entire downstairs is void of people. Inside the kitchen, a pot of water heats on the stove.

The back stairs in the kitchen lead to Ruby's private rooms in the house.

The scent of burning sage greets me. Ruby's door to her room hangs open. Inside, she's on her knees, her elbows on the bed. I hear her crying, see the two basins on the floor not far from her.

While I can't hear what she says, I know she's praying. Getting down on my knees beside her, covering my hands over her cool ones, she startles and looks over at me.

"Jolene Willow Dean, you about gave me a heart attack." There's a wan smile on those lips. Strands of hair fall from her bun, and her apron has stains. Her eyes are watery and dark circles blemish her pale skin.

"I'm sorry, Ruby. I had to come see if you were well. The doctor's wife told me about the food poisoning. Why didn't you send someone to fetch me? I would have been here to help."

"There is no one to send. Robbie's down with it, too. Chord set him to your room. I'm sorry, Jo. You can't come back until we get over this."

Ruby struggled to get to her feet. Holding her by the elbow, I help her. "Do you know what caused it? The doctor's wife didn't say. I thought it was the biscuits from the hotel. I tried to get Daphne to confess after seeing her slipping one to Mr. Conway."

Ruby grabs for the post on her bed. "Jensen admitted to selling us all moldy flour. It's the weather, he said. Benjamin made him dump it even though the doctor confirmed it was the salted pork." Ruby pants, her head bending.

"Maybe you should lie down," I try to guide her down on the bed.

"No, Jo. There are sick people in my home. I've got water boiling, basins to clean," she sits on the bed.

"I've got this." I take her hands again as she sits. "You took care of me and taught me to keep a house. Let me return the favor. I couldn't bear it if something happened to you," my voice chokes with emotion. "The doctor says it will pass. I'll get you water. You need to stay hydrated, and you'll be back on your feet in no time."

"Maybe I'll rest for a moment. I've been on my feet all night." She lays back, her eyes drifting close.

"Don't you worry, Ruby, I've got this," I say.

Shedding my coat and hat, I leave them hanging in the kitchen. Outside, I carry in water, heat it, let it cool, and take a pitcher from room to room to ensure everyone has a freshwater glass. The stench down the hall could cause the toughest cowgirl to gag.

Knocking on each door before I enter. The gambler's room is empty. Across the hall, Mr. Clark moans.

Out of all the boarders, the elderly couple received the worse of it. Inside my room, Robbie sits on the bed, the sheets the same as I left them after my big splash. Sitting on the corner of the bed is the gambler, dealing out another card to the boy.

"Jolene, darlin', come join us. This is your room, is it not?" He's without his jacket or his vest. His shirt buttons have a few undone, letting a vee open at the neck over his chest. His boots are missing, but his hands are as quick in shuffling as I've ever seen them.

"Blackjack, Jo?" Robbie asks.

"Does your mother know you're sick or you're gambling?" I ask, walking around the bed and taking a seat on the other corner of the bed.

"Doc said he'd send word to my Ma. He's headed out there to check on Mrs. Dawson."

"That's good. I pick up the cards dealt to me."

"I say we make this interesting," the gambler grins.

"Mr. Weston is a pro. He's going to teach me to be a pro, too," Robbie says. "He's been down the Mississippi on one of the riverboats."

"I think I remember hearing something about it." I look at my cards, not believing I'm doing this. "No stakes," I point at him. "This is a friendly game."

"You heard the woman," the gambler winks at Robbie.

We play a good ole hand of poker, the gambler taking the time to spread out his cards and teach Robbie the different hands, helping him win this hand and several others. I go about the house, checking on everyone, seeing to the kitchen, and going returning to my room.

The longer we play, I find myself stretched out on the bed, belly down.

The time comes when Robbie must lie down his cards. I go to check on the others again. Ruby's sawing logs in her sleep. Down in the kitchen, I head out on the porch to grab the sheets. Since the rain let up, Ruby hung out freshly washed sheets. Where this woman found the energy, I'll never know.

Outside, the sheets billow in the breeze. I'm about to take them off the line as another pair of hands joins mine. The scent washes over me. Sweet tobacco teases my senses. The zings going down my arms at his touch can take a girl's breath away.

The bounty hunter's thumb rubs over my bruised knuckles. "Something I should know about?"

Slipping my hand out from under his, I pull the sheet down and fold it the best I can. "I didn't hit anyone if that's what you're wondering."

"Your hair looks nice. I'm glad you let Minnie help you."

Biting my lip, I give him the eye. "Where you been?"

"Helping the sheriff. If Brody was in town, he's gone now."

Walking back into the kitchen, I ask, "You going to go after him?"

The bounty hunter fills the frame of the doorway. "What do you think, Dimples?"

That would be a yes. Laying the sheets on a counter, I check on the water boiling. "Conway had food poisoning."

"I know, the sheriff told me."

"Of course, he did." Down the hall, I hear the shuffle of feet. "Anything else you came here to tell me?"

"If I didn't know better, I'd say this suits you," he moves around me, grabbing the metal coffee pot and pouring in some of the hot water I've been heating nonstop all afternoon.

"Chasing killers? You could say I get that from hanging out with you."

He pulls out the coffee. "I meant tending to others, helping Ruby here, and keeping house."

"Are you complimenting me on my wifely skills?" I decide to get saucy with him.

From the other doorway, the gambler snorts. "And which skills would those be?"

The bounty hunter narrows his eyes on the gambler. "You mind, Weston. My wife and I are having a private conversation."

"By all means." the gambler steps further inside. "From what we've all seen and heard, there's nothing private about your marriage?"

I suck in my breath.

"What do you need, Weston?" The bounty hunter stays between us. He finishes making coffee.

"The youngin' ruined my cards and his sheets, or I should yours," the gambler eases against the wall. His hair appears more mused than earlier. The ends glint red in the late afternoon sun bleeding through the window.

"Robbie. I'll go see to him." I don't give either man a chance to say more. Grabbing the sheets I brought in, I head down the hall. Passing the parlor, I spot the elderly man sitting in a chair and staring out the window at the street. "How are you feeling?"

He gazes over at me, his eyes watering. "I could use something solid in my stomach," he says.

"I'll see what I can do. Give me a few moments. Is your wife well?"

"Make no mistake, my Mildred is a strong woman. She holds her convictions just as strong."

"Living out here, I suppose a woman has to hold her own and then some."

He smiles, not quite to his eyes. "We were young too, once.

Sometimes I think she forgets it. Seeing you and your husband reminds a man of what living is like."

While I might have gone speechless, my face warms. Of course, nothing is happening between the bounty hunter and me behind closed doors, but the man makes a good show for everyone else.

"Are you settling in Deadwood or heading somewhere else?" The sheets in my arms remind me Robbie is waiting.

"Had a claim up in the hills, but Mildred wanted civilization. Life is hard. She's lived through six babies and burying four. When the bank man came through offering to buy our claim, Mildred begged me to take the offer. So I did. We've got a daughter to the north. We plan on spending the rest of our years settling there."

"The bank? Not the railroad?" I ask.

"Heard they were coming through, but Mildred wouldn't hold out. She wanted gone from the hills. Not another winter she threatened me."

"It was a fair offer?" I ask.

The man's face twists. "There's nothing fair about the bank's threat. It was sell out or pay up in full. The man is a weasel. You got land there. You and your husband beware."

"Thank you for the warning. I've got to take care of these. Then when I come back down, we'll see about getting you something solid to eat."

Down the hall, I spot the gambler heading my way. I point to the parlor. He puts on one of those deep dimple grins, but his eyes are dull from the toll of the sickness. "You know, darlin', you want to keep practicing those wifely skills. I'd be happy to help."

Scowling at him, I head for the stairs. After I get Robbie settled, I've got some settling of my own to do.

Starting with a certain bank owner.

19

Other than finding out about the food poisoning, the bounty hunter spent the day with the sheriff tracking the leader of the Brownell gang. With new campsites outside town filled with rail workers, the men could have moved on or blended in with the influx of strangers.

One thing we both find strange is the sheriff hiring Payne. I don't point out that if the bounty hunter had taken the job, the sheriff wouldn't have had to take the first able body he found.

I whip up some bread and broth from the pantry in Ruby's boarding house. Checking on her, I leave Ruby a note, a pitcher, and a glass of water and cover her up before I go.

"Maybe I should stay here for the night," I say as the bounty hunter hands me my jacket for us to go.

"Weston and some others are feeling better. You can come back over in the morning."

There won't be anywhere for me to sleep with Robbie in my room except the couch in the living area. I'm okay with that, but he's not by the looks of the bounty hunter.

Inside the hotel, Sherman grimaces at the sight of us. "What are you doing back here?"

"I believe we have a room here," I say.

"There a problem?" the bounty hunter asks.

Sherman stands up straight, staying behind his counter. "Mr. Warner has decided you are no longer welcome to stay at this hotel."

"Is that so?" The bounty hunter's eyebrows draw together. "Care to tell us why?"

Sherman scratches the side of his neck. "I believe it has to do with your wife's behavior toward another guest."

The bounty hunter gives me a sidelong glance. I shrug.

"Miss Davenport," Sherman says, gaining a bit of smugness.

"What does Miss Davenport have to do with anything?" the bounty hunter is looking at me now. "Jo?"

"I may have thought she tried to poison Mr. Conway, and she took offense."

His brows shot straight up.

"A misunderstanding." I give a pointed look at Sherman. "One which I apologized for didn't happen here in the hotel and isn't anyone else's concern."

"I see." The bounty hunter says. I do not like the way he says it or how he looks from me to Sherman.

Turning my back to Sherman, I whisper furiously, giving the bounty hunter the low down of what happened. My heart sinks, and I feel bad enough without having to keep repeating.

He cups his hand over his mouth, his gaze on Sherman. Finished with my explanation, he lands a hand on my shoulder. "From now on, you come to me with your theories first."

"I could," I mutter, "If you're ever around."

He gives my shoulder a squeeze, and I avoid looking at him.

"I believe whatever misunderstanding between my wife and

Miss Davenport is no concern of the hotel. We'll be heading to our room."

The bounty hunter turns me, takes my arm, and we head for the stairs. Sherman races around the counter, blocking us from the stairs. For a man who doesn't do much all day, he can sure move fast.

"Mr. Warner has banned your wife from the hotel for as long as the Davenports are in residence."

Well, it wouldn't be long. Daphne told me her father was searching for a house for them to rent.

"I paid for the week," the bounty hunter says. "You prepared to reimburse me for the remaining days?"

Sherman stutters. I almost pity him. "Mr. Warner said…."

"Where is Mr. Warner?" the bounty hunter asks.

"He's in his office, with Mr. Davenport, I believe."

"Good. Stay here, Jo. I need to have a word with Warner." He grabs me by the chin, forcing me to look him in the eye. "Don't go anywhere without me."

Crossing my arms, I say, "Fine."

He swipes his thumb across my cheek. "Good girl."

Sherman tries to talk the bounty hunter into leaving and coming back later, but the bounty hunter is made of stone. He's unmovable. Sherman follows him, glancing several times at me. Worry furrows the lanky man's face.

Once he's gone, I lean against the counter, waiting. Inside my pocket, the key to my room heats against my palm. I fiddle with it around against my palm.

The bounty hunter asked me to stay here. No, he told me. I chew on my lip when I hear Daphne's voice at the top of the stairs.

Maybe if I have another word with her, this will get all cleared up faster. Why should I apologize again?

I can't keep having the bounty hunter cover my tracks or

fishing me out of trouble. No, I take the stairs, deciding to settle this maturely between women.

The closer I get, the more heated Daphne's voice sounds. Coming up around the corner of the stairs to the landing, I spy Harris with his hand curled around Daphne's arm.

"I'm going to tell my father."

Harris pushes her back against the wall. "Tell him anything you like. We both know he's got you sold off. You do as I say, and I'll have you on a train back east attending parties with all your lady friends, or did your father sell the townhouse, too?"

Daphne reaches up to slap him, but Harris grips her wrist, pulling her hand toward his mouth. His lips caress the inside of her palm. Making a fist, I realize I have the same reaction as Daphne.

"You're no better than the filthy scout Thomas hired. How dare you threaten me?"

Harris bends his head, drawing her closer. "I took care of Coose, and I'll take care of anyone in my way. Shame, you've got such a pretty neck." Harris jerks on her wrist, taking his other hand to trail a finger down her exposed throat. Daphne turns her head away, her eyes widening as she spots me.

Staying at the corner of the landing, Harris hasn't noticed me, but as soon as he says, "Your father will have no choice but to hand all the decisions over to me once you're gone. He'll be distraught with grief, and with Conway in jail, there will be no one to oppose me." I take a step further into the hallway.

"H-how do you s-suppose to get r-rid of me?" Daphne asks.

"A trip down the stairs should do it." Grabbing her by the throat, he twists her around, shoving her towards the stairs. Daphne screams, "Jo Dee, help me!"

Harris keeps his hold on Daphne, pulling out his gun to aim at me. Daphne struggles, her fingers clawing at the hand around her throat. He squeezes, cutting off her air. "Make another noise, and I'll kill you," he says, "And her."

The gun pointed at me doesn't scare me as much as watching Daphne gasp for breath.

"Let her go," I say.

"How much did you hear?" he asks.

"You're planning on taking Daphne on a trip?" Okay, maybe those weren't his exact words. "You should let her go. It'll take her two days to pack with all the dresses she has in her trunk."

"Shut up," Harris pulls the hammer back. I've never been one to pee my pants, but death staring you in the face can bring on the sudden urge. "Where's that husband of yours?"

"I left him at the boarding house," I raise my hands, lying through my teeth. "You might have heard. Food poison has got them all confined to their rooms."

"I warned Davenport that skipping on the vitals would cause problems. Good thing the mercantile was more than happy to take it off our hands in trade from some dry tack."

Daphne's lips are turning blue. Her eyes roll up to the whites.

"Let her go. She can't breathe," I take a step forward, and he jerks her back.

"No husband. No Daddy to save you," he glances down at Daphne. "No witnesses."

"You don't want to shoot us. The sound will have everyone downstairs running again." Which would be a good thing if the gun wasn't pointed directly at me.

Harris nods, forcing Daphne forward. He keeps the gun trained on me. "It won't look good if one of you goes and not the other."

Relaxing his grip on Daphne's neck, she gasps, taking in gulps of air.

"You don't have to do this," I say. "You told Daphne you took care of Coose. He won't bother her anymore. You've got

Conway framed for the murder. Why not marry her instead of killing her? You'd gain money and control."

Harris looks menacing. "Stupid woman. I didn't kill Coose because he insulted this twit. Happens things that night fell right into place in my favor. Coose promised me part of the split, then tried to cheat me."

"You shot him."

"He shouldn't have tried to pull his gun on me," Harris says. "Then Conway comes knocking on the door. It was self-defense."

"Then why run and let Conway take the fall?" Silently, I pray for the bounty hunter, Sherman, anyone to come down the hall or up those stairs.

"It got him out of the way."

"Killer," Daphne shrieks.

Harris presses his hand tighter against Daphne's neck, making her go quiet. I shake my head in her direction, hoping to buy us more time.

I need to make a habit of carrying Shorty wherever I go. Standing defenseless sends cold drips of fear down a cowgirl's spine.

"With Conway out of the way, you get to take his place. Mr. Davenport is a money man. He knows nothing about tracks and trains."

"And here I thought you were stupid," he grunts as Daphne tries to stomp his foot

"With the contracts on the land rerouting the tracks, a man can accommodate enough money to live well."

"I think it's time for me to bid you ladies goodnight," Harris says.

Daphne's eyes go as wide as an owl. Harris's hand squeezes tighter, his gun hand drops slightly, and I take the moment to lunge toward him. Forcing him back a step or two is all I need to put him off balance and yank Daphne from his grasp. He raises the gun right at her, and I do the only thing I can.

I pull her back against me. Harris reaches again for her neck. The stairs are closer than I thought. My foot slips on the landing, trying to twist to dodge his attempt to get Daphne. Daphne screams and grabs the first thing she can grasp, as the wooden stairs are the first to hit my back. Harris comes rolling down the entire flight with us in a mess of tangled limbs, and Daphne's vocals alert everyone in the hotel better than a fireman's bell.

Sherman shouts at the bottom of the stairs, but we take him out in the spill. Both Daphne and I land atop Harris, who lands on top of Sherman.

Pain shots through my hip and across my back. Daphne hasn't stopped screaming, and I'm not moving. There is no way I'm letting Harris get up until the sheriff gets here.

Closing my eyes against the burning pain in my back, I tell Daphne, "Stop screaming."

"Get off me!" she sobs. "Help me!"

A pair of hands pull me off. Daphne stops screaming, turning into sobs, and I join her. Looking up at the bounty hunter, I cry, "Put me down!"

He drops me on the floor beside him. Nausea rises in my stomach. Dizziness wavers my sight. I think that's Warner plucking Daphne off Harris.

"She tried to kill me," Daphne clings to Warner.

"He did it," I say to the bounty hunter. "Harris confessed. He killed Coose, framed Conway, and he was going to kill Daphne when I found him in the hall upstairs."

Harris rolls over, cursing, reaching for his gun, to find an unconscious Sherman beneath him. The bounty hunter pulls his weapon, "You're under arrest, Harris."

"The wife of yours is crazy," Harris hisses. "She tried to kill us. Arrest her."

Davenport grabs Daphne from Warner. "Why are you standing here? This is your hotel. Go get the sheriff!"

Daphne sobs into her father's chest. Her hair has come out of its fancy updo. She wails as more staff and the few guests staying at the hotel enter the foyer to see the commotion. "Don't stand there gawking," Davenport billows. "Fetch a doctor. My daughter is hurt."

The bounty hunter lets Harris struggle to his feet before clamping him on the shoulder and keeping his six-shooter at his back.

"Jo?"

"Lock him away," I say, laying back on the floor, staring up at the ceiling. What's a cowgirl to do after she's taken a tumble down the stairs?

Reaching up, I pat my head, my neck. At least those aren't broken. Not a hair has come out of place from Minnie's hard work this morning. The woman knows how to put in some tight braids.

While I lay there, Davenport and several staff fuss over Daphne, and some other people check on Sherman. The man is on his back, there's no blood, and someone confirms he's breathing.

The sheriff arrives with Warner to take everyone's statements. Soon the bounty hunter returns after Harris is locked behind bars.

"Arrest her too, sheriff!" Davenport points his finger at me. "She tried to get my daughter killed."

"It's her fault we fell down the stairs," Daphne sobs again. "I think my leg is broken."

To Davenport's great dismay, the doctor's wife rushes into the hotel foyer, ignoring Daphne. The woman focuses on Sherman first.

"My daughter is in pain," Davenport gets angry.

"At least she's awake and tells us what is hurting," the

doctor's wife says. She glances over at me, still lying flat on my back. "Can you get up?"

I shake my head. It hurts to breathe as my lungs try to expand. There is fire crawling up my spine and over my hip. This is worse, Lulu dragging me through town. More than the time, I got thrown from one of Chitto's ponies racing through the hills when we were younger. I always had to prove I could keep up and that I was worthy of being a part of their tribe. Tears sting in my eyes.

Crouched beside me, the bounty hunter takes my hand. "Where does it hurt, Jo?"

"Everywhere," I tell him. "Please let me go home," I whisper.

The sheriff asks me a few questions, and I tell him what happened in order to keep him distracted from the pain radiating through my body. Once, my father, Earl, had to shoot our mule to put it out of its misery. I'm about halfway there.

Soon, the doctor's wife instructs Warner, and with the help of the sheriff and the bounty hunter, they put Sherman in his room at the hotel. The doctor will have to take a better look at him when he gets back, but the wife feels Sherman hit his head when he landed a little too hard. She's not sure if or when he'll wake up.

All eyes turn to me. It's not my fault. Daphne is the next to get checked out. Warner practically carries her to her room with Mr. Davenport.

He looks down his nose at me, and I close my eyes, not wanting my last memory of a scowling, portly man glaring down his nose at me.

Once my ribs are down to an ache, and the burn doesn't spread further, I push up. Groaning, I struggle to sit up, but the bounty hunter stops me. "You need to let the doctor's wife look at you."

"It doesn't matter." I look at her. "No offense." Then back at the bounty hunter. "She can't fix what's broken, anyway."

The bounty hunter frowns. Turns out I can't stand. The pain is too bad, and sitting up takes my breath away.

Warner tries to deny me staying in the room the bounty hunter rented, but the sheriff points out I caught a killer and saved another victim. If only Daphne and the others saw it that way.

Regardless, the bounty hunter helps me to our room, along with the sheriff and the doctor's wife. She offers me medicine to take away the pain. The bounty hunter tries to convince me. Maybe I'm more like the mule my father put down than I want to admit. I don't take the medicine. I don't trust it. The last saloon owner, Glen, tried to put me to sleep, permanently, with the stuff.

She leaves some with the bounty hunter, and it's a long night of lying awake on my back in bed. The bounty hunter sits on the bed beside me, a pillow tucked against his back. He keeps his six-shooter across his lap and his boots crossed. If anyone comes into our room during the night, they'll have to get past him first.

20

The entire town is in a fray of activity. Begrudgingly, Warner agreed to leave me stay in the hotel until the doctor gave me the okay to get out of bed.

Ruby has come over each day to sit a spell with me in the afternoons. The boarding house residents have all recovered, and the elder couple left on the stage yesterday afternoon.

The bounty hunter brought me pie and sandwiches from the diner down the street. I can honestly say I'm one spoiled cowgirl.

Minnie has come every day to help me wash and do my hair. After a week of fussing, I'm back in the green floral dress. Lucky me, Minnie went easy on lacing the corset. My entire body is every color, from deep purple to sickly yellow.

Mr. Conway is a man of his word. He paid the bounty hunter the agreed sum. Packing my few belongings in the hotel, I allow the bounty hunter to walk me down the stairs. I wince with each step.

"You sure you're okay, Dimples?" he asks, keeping at my side while I slide my hand down the polish rail. "Fine." It's not the physical pain so much as the memory of these stairs causing me to flinch.

I don't realize I'm holding my breath until we're down at the bottom.

Sherman is absent from the desk. Warner keeps a respectful distance. He taps his fingers on the hotel log, and I feel he wants to say something. I stop by the desk while the bounty hunter turns in our key.

"You owe me for three extra nights," Warner says. "The room service was on the house."

I'd ask what room service. Considering the bounty hunter brought me food, Minnie kept the room clean, and it's not like anyone brought us fresh linens.

Without a word, the bounty hunter pulls out the required amount, tossing it on the ledger in front of Warner.

"Our nightly game is moving over to the saloon tomorrow if you're in." Warner slides the money from sight.

Looking between him and the bounty hunter, I gingerly move toward the door. Before I can grab the knob, the bounty hunter is there. "We need to stop in at Osterloh's office before going to the church."

As soon as the cool May breeze touches my face, I pull my jacket closer around me. "Unusual weather, isn't it, Miss?" a man says in passing.

"It's cool for May," I reply.

The bounty hunter keeps his hand on my back. The warmth sends tingles up my spine.

Osterloh's office is on another side street inside a two-story house. His study has rows of bookshelves and dull dark wood. The armed chair he occupies is the deepest of greens. He doesn't bother standing when his daughter ushers us into the room. She's a middle-aged woman with children racing around on the floor above us. It seems everyone is in a tizzy about the festival today.

Sitting in a chair to our left, the gambler turns his head with a grin. "Jolene, darlin', you're back on your feet."

He stands. "Please take my chair."

"I'll stand, thank you." Getting up and down makes my hip scream with protest. There is no use aggravating it any more than I need.

"Mr. And Mrs. Townes." Osterloh gets right to the point. "Since Mr. Weston is here, we have a matter of signing over the deed. Mr. Reed has kindly supplied me with a copy of the banknote showing you've paid your debt."

"We could have waited until Monday. I'm sorry you have to deal with this matter today, Mr. Osterloh. I know many folks are eager to head to the church for the festival."

"We don't have until Monday." Today is the last day to settle the matter of my land per the judge's time limit, and Weston knows it.

One more day and I wouldn't be able to buy him out.

"I have to admit, I'm surprised to see you here," Osterloh clears his throat. "We'd best settle this matter before the sheriff comes to collect you."

"Collect me?" Panic rises in my chest. My ribs throb, and the corset isn't helping any.

"Davenport is pressing charges against you for attempted murder," the bounty hunter says calmly, asking for someone to pass the salt at dinner.

"He can't do that, can he?" My mind races, going over the possibilities. "How long have you known?"

"The sheriff isn't coming to arrest you," the bounty hunter lands his deadly stare on the attorney.

"I believe Miss Davenport testified that you pulled her down the stairs," the gambler says, not helping in this situation.

"There is no law broken," the bounty hunter tries to assure me. "Besides, you got Harris's confession, and by what he told the sheriff, it was all an accident."

"It was an accident, wasn't it, Jolene?" the gambler asks, concern crossing his features.

"Of course!" I say.

The gambler puts up his hands in defense. "We are in an attorney's office, just saying." He tilts his head toward Mr. Osterloh, who appears to be about to fall asleep.

"Let's get this done so I can have my land back."

The gambler shrugs. "Have it your way. When your husband takes off and leaves you all alone, don't you worry, darlin', I am not going anywhere."

"You're not leaving?"

Why does the thought of him leaving burrow a hole inside of me? It's the dimples. No, it's those green eyes. Or maybe's it's the way those brown locks of hair glint red in the sunlight that entrance me?

"Why would I leave?" the gambler finishes signing where the attorney points out to him.

"Don't you have a riverboat to catch?" the bounty hunter asks.

"Let's say thanks to this here payoff, I'm now in a position to make a business investment. What can I say? Deadwood has grown on me."

Taking the pen, dipping the end in the ink pot, I scribble my name to ensure Tail Feather's and Chitto's tribe stay hidden.

With the paperwork finished, I say, "While you enjoy your stay, I'll be heading back to my mountain home."

"One more signature." Osterloh holds out the pen and his hand trembles. "Mr. Townes."

My brows furrow. "What does he have to sign for?"

"He's your husband," Osterloh says.

The gambler chuckles. "What's yours is his." He leans closer to me. "Law says he oversees your property. What do you get from him?" The gambler makes a face, and I try hard not to show my dismay. "You sure you have a claim to go back to?"

"What's that supposed to mean?" I ask.

The bounty hunter signs the papers. "Nothing, Jo. Go on your way, Weston. We're finished here."

"You'd make a terrible poker player," the gambler says. "Your husband is hiding something from you."

Weston leaves, and I hug myself, waiting for Osterloh to hand the bounty hunter the finalized papers or signed document from him stating the debt and land claim have been settled. The bounty hunter tucks them inside his duster. "I'll see you get these when we return to the boarding house."

The attorney's daughter herds her three children out the door before us on our way out. They race down the street.

"What do we do now?" I ask.

"We go to the festival." The bounty hunter takes my hand and places it at the bend of his arm.

"I meant about my claim and your name on it." Do I have to spell it out for him?

"Is there a problem? We're married. The law states a man has the right to oversee his wife's property."

Silence falls between us as I quietly contemplate my next steps. "And when we're not married anymore?"

The bounty hunter doesn't miss a step. "You trying to get rid of me, Dimples?"

"No." I choose my words carefully, not wanting to reveal more than my feelings than I want him to see. "But what if you meet someone and want to marry her one day?"

"Are you sure that's what's on your mind?" he asks, looking straight ahead.

"Well, say I meet someone, and I want a proper marriage. You said this was in name only, but maybe someday I'll want some kids and a husband who will build me a white picket fence."

He tenses as we come to the end of the street. We turn going down Main Street in the direction of the church.

The gambler is right. I have a terrible poker face.

"When you meet the man, you let me know. If he's a good man, I'll let you go, but I am keeping my ten percent," he says.

A deal is a deal. I offered the bounty hunter ten percent of my claim share to help find my father's killer. I still have ninety percent.

"So, we're going to keep pretending?" I ask.

His hand covers mine. Little zings snake up my wrist and arm. "I don't trust Weston. I wouldn't put it past him to have the judge annual our partnership."

Nearing the church, I spy Ella Mae over by the food table. There is a wagon in the schoolyard with men setting up to play their fiddles and guitars. Someone has piled wood off to the side for a fire. It reminds me of when Chitto pulled me into dancing around the firelight at one of his tribe's celebrations.

I thought I loved him back then, and maybe I do. Not in the same way as when we were young.

"Partners?" I ask. "Is that what we are?"

The bounty hunter reaches in his duster for a cigar. "What else would we be, Dimples?"

My breath hitches. The bounty hunter pulls a match from that same pocket, striking it against the side of a wagon parked with a line of others. He lights his cigar, and my hand falls away.

He gives me a questioning look, but I can't answer him. Because honestly, I don't know.

"I think I see Ruby. I should go say hello."

The bounty stays near the wagon, smoking his cigar. Ladies have lined tables filled with fried chicken, baked potatoes, pies, cakes, and a dozen other fixings for the celebration. Everyone in town has come out this afternoon for the festival.

There are picnic baskets lined up the stairs to the church.

It's not long before Hannah Baker is standing between them all at the top of the stairs with Mr. Reed from the bank and the mayor of Deadwood, Hayward Tooker.

Hannah keeps a hand on his arm, introducing him as she shouts to make sure everyone can hear her. "Mr. Reed is going to be our auctioneer. Now, if I can have each lady come and claim her basket. Gentleman, you'll be bidding on the basket," she teeters off into a giggle, "and the company of the woman who put the time and effort into making it for you."

I notice Ruby hasn't gone to pick up a basket. "I thought all the single ladies made baskets."

Ruby points under the sawhorses, where they've made a make-shift table with boards for the food. "No one would buy my basket."

She's got on a frilly blouse and a dark-colored skirt. Her hair is twisted in the back, and a small braid leads into it from each side. I don't have to ask if Minnie got a hold of her.

"You don't know for certain. What about Sheriff Bentley?"

I wiggle my eyebrows at her. She laughs, patting my arm. "I am too old for that kind of nonsense."

"Pfft…" Amaryllis comes strutting across the yard. "Ruby Hazelton, there is no such thing when it comes to finding the right man."

I missed seeing her the night we stayed at the ranch. It would appear Buck has been a good influence on the former saloon matron.

"I had a man, bless his soul, my Henry. Sometimes all we get is once, and once is enough." Ruby rubs her arms. "It's brisk for May. I think I left my jacket inside the church. I'll be right back."

Amaryllis walks over and picks up the basket.

"That's Ruby's."

"It's a shame to let her good cooking go to waste," Amaryllis looks inside. "She even wrapped up two honey buns.

Robbie said how you helped take care of him, you and Mr. Weston." She gazes out amongst the people crowding around the church stairs.

"How is he doing?" I ask.

Amaryllis narrows her gaze. "He can go back to work for Jensen on Monday."

"You're not taking him back to the ranch?"

Amaryllis wraps her arms around the basket. "He's better off here. He's got a roof over his head, food in his belly, and no one making him scrub his fingers to the bone."

Before I can say more, she walks away. "Ruby's basket deserves to be auctioned off."

"I agree, but she's not going to take it up there," I say.

I notice Amaryllis has gloves covering her hands. "I heard about your accident on the stairs. It's probably better for me to take it." She winks and takes off.

Reed is halfway through auctioning off the baskets. Amaryllis doesn't wait. She marches right past all the other women, right past Hannah Baker, in charge of the ladies standing in front to show off what's inside their baskets.

Ruby comes out, and I move closer. Weston stands in the crowd, and the gambler leans back, watching it all from the side of a wagon with his favorite cigar.

Hannah gets flustered, trying to make Amaryllis go to the back of the line. She hisses in the saloon matron's face. This auction is for food and nothing else.

The hard set of Amaryllis's gaze causes the crowd to cluster closer. Naturally, there is nothing better than an old-fashioned slap contest to perk the crowd's interest.

I can't see the big deal. Emma and Eva Swanson are in line, as is my mother, Polly. They, too, are at the back of the line.

Hannah picks up her basket. It's got a bow that matches her dress. "I was going to go next."

"You can wait for one more person," Amaryllis says. She holds out her basket and puts on a flashy smile for all the men. Batting her lashes, she announces, "Who wants to get their hands on some delicious honey buns?"

The bidding starts with a cowhand and a railroad worker, upping each other every turn. Buck comes rushing through the yard, past the wagons, and the crowd parts for him, almost like Reverend Carter's story about Moses and the red sea.

By the determined look on his face, I'd gather Buck isn't too happy about some other man having a picnic with his woman.

"Amaryllis," Buck warns, "Where did you get that basket?"

"None of your business." Turning her head, she keeps smiling at the men's bidding. She drops her shoulder. While clothed more than I'm used to seeing her, she curls those lips up, and the bids drive higher.

"You're not single. This auction is for single ladies," Buck says.

"I tried to tell her," Hannah says.

Reed keeps the bidding going. Buck tells him to stop, but they're well over a few dollars for Ruby's basket.

"Do you see me with a wedding ring or a marriage certificate?" she glares at him.

"That's not the point," he growls.

"What is the point?" the gambler asks. "I believe the woman is trying to help raise funds for the new courthouse."

"I am." Amaryllis pouts. "You gonna bid on my basket or stand there and let some other man take me on a picnic?"

Buck huffs but tosses his hand in for the next bid. His eyes lock on hers, and the heat waves ripple through the crowd.

Even the bounty hunter has left his stance by the wagon, snuffing out his cigar and coming to stand beside me. On the other side, Ruby joins me. "What is going on?"

"No sense in wasting a good basket," I repeat what Amaryllis said.

"She shouldn't have done that," Ruby huffed. "I planned for you and Chord to take it."

The bounty hunter throws his hand into the bid. After a while, it's him against Buck.

"You've got a woman. Why are you trying to take mine?" Buck keeps his hand in the bid.

"All I'm after is the basket," the bounty hunter nods, keeping the bid going.

After a point, Buck winces and puts his hand down.

Amaryllis stomps her foot. "You gonna let him have it?"

"He can have the basket." Buck yanks the item in question from Amaryllis. "You're going back to the ranch with me."

Chord wins the bid. He steps up to take the basket, and Hannah intercepts him. She makes a show of her basket is compared to Ruby's. "You don't find that one to your liking, Mr. Townes. I assure you I'm an excellent cook. I've got cobbler, freshly baked bread, and berry preserves."

"I'm sure any man here will be lucky to sample it and your company," the bounty hunter says.

Hannah's scowl goes ignored. In the distance, Buck has Amaryllis by the arm, dragging her toward where the horses, buggies, and wagons are parked. She yanks away from him, yelling at him. Buck yells back. It's hard to make out their argument with Reed starting the bid on Hannah's basket.

The bounty hunter invites Ruby to join us and teases her about eating her own food, but she takes it in good humor.

Things get heated between Buck and Amaryllis. "Hold this," the bounty hunter pushes the basket in my arms. He lengthens his stride, heading for the couple. Amaryllis reaches back and slaps Buck. He balls his hands into a fist, but the bounty hunter stands between them before he can launch at her.

Amaryllis screams and dashes toward the street. Buck picks up his fallen hat. His hands wave every which way as he tells the bounty hunter to stay out of his business.

With the show over, the crowd goes back to bidding on the ladies' baskets. Folk split for a while, some mingling and eating from the spread the married ladies have put out to share. Folks mingle in the schoolyard, and some are further into the trees and behind the church, where couples sit with their baskets sharing food and conversation.

The bounty hunter and I stand behind the wagon, Ruby's spread laid out in front of us.

"We can find a place under the trees," the bounty hunter offers.

"And sit on the hard, cold ground? No thanks," I pluck a honey bun before he takes them both.

The honey bun is plucked from my hand, about to take a bite. "Someone like you doesn't deserve something so sweet."

21

"I saved your life." I pluck the honeybun right back out of Daphne Davenport's hand. "You're welcome."

Daphne glowers at me. She's got a crutch under one arm, and Mr. Conway holding her on the other. On her crouch side, her father stands, his chest puffed out.

I take a bite of my honeybun.

"Your reckless behavior almost cost my daughter her life," Davenport says.

Ruby snickers. "A twisted ankle is far from a broken neck or lying unconscious like poor Sherman."

"Sherman Ferrell is the one who deserves the thanks. He stepped in and tried to save my daughter." Davenport touches Daphne on the arm. She bats her pretty lashes, and I don't have to turn to see the gambler heading our way.

"You'd rather give a man in the wrong place at the wrong time credit than acknowledge a woman avoided anyone getting killed," I say, probably needing to stuff more honeybun in my mouth before starting more trouble.

Mr. Conway interjects. "You got the killer and the reward. You, therefore, have my thanks."

His words humble me, and the ire in my bloodstream calms. Or maybe it's the rush of the sweet honey flowing through my veins.

"Either way, your wife has left us without a foreman, in addition to not having a scout. Mr. Townes, I am here to inform you our deal is off unless you change your mind and scout for the rest of the rail line for us," Davenport says.

The bounty hunter's brow furrows. I take a step back. Those cold-stone eyes of his land on Davenport. "My wife caught the man who killed your scout and freed your partner. I'd say we're even."

"Your wife tried to kill my daughter!" Davenport goes red in the face.

The gambler comes up beside him looking amused.

"If I wanted to kill her, I would have pushed her down the stairs, not tumbled down them with her!"

The bounty hunter steps in front of me while the gambler steps in front of both the Davenports.

"Now, now." The gambler holds up his hands. "I think we got a misunderstanding here. Nothing to go pulling out lead over." His gaze falls to the bounty hunter's hand, poised over his six-shooter.

"Scouting for you wasn't part of our deal," the bounty hunter says. "I have other business to attend that doesn't involve land negotiations."

"Well understood," Mr. Conway covers Daphne's hand over his arm. Her black tresses are twisted in a knot at the back of her neck. Those lavender eyes throw darts in my direction.

"However, without a scout to get us through the mountains, we won't be able to complete our pass, and our deal won't be valid."

"This is non-negotiable," Davenport adds.

Conway frowns at him. "I believe what my associate is saying is that until we replace Coose and Harris, we will be forced to keep camping around town and in the Black Hills, costing us time and money."

I suppose this is a pickle for the Davenports. Daphne said her father has invested in the railroad to the hilt. I can't stop feeling bad for them both.

Still, the woman has no right to say I tried to kill her. "What deal are we talking about?"

"Yes, I'd be interested in knowing as well," says the gambler.

"This doesn't concern you, Weston," the bounty hunter says.

"The deal your husband made with us to secure your land and proceed with the tracks going through as planned," Davenport informs me.

"Why don't you take Daphne to get a drink and find a place to sit? I'm sure she's exhausted from the excursion for us to join the festivities. Mr. Townes, Mrs. Townes," Conway inclines his head. "Perhaps we could take a walk?"

"I think that is an excellent idea," Ruby pipes up. "Mr. Weston can assist Daphne in Mr. Conway's place, and we'll go see about finding a suitable spot to watch the festivities."

A light comes forth in Daphne's eyes. "Yes, please assist me, Mr. Weston. I would be so grateful."

Sliding closer to the bounty hunter, I take his arm. "A walk is a lovely idea," I smile over at Daphne. She can thank me later.

"I see no reason why I should go too," Davenport is as stubborn as a mule. "Send the ladies with Mr. Weston, and we men can settle our business."

"This is Jo's business, too," the bounty hunter says. "I don't think you should stay. I don't appreciate the hostility you've displayed toward my wife."

"He's right, David. This is railroad business. I don't need you as part of this meeting," Conway dismisses him.

Davenport pinches his lips together. Conway stares at him. Finally, Davenport doesn't even offer to aid Daphne as he stalks away.

The gambler loops Daphne's hand into his arm. "Let's see about getting you some refreshment. I'm told there will be dancing soon and some games to watch."

"I take it I'm finally going to find out what you've been conspiring about behind my back?" I ask.

All this business of finding Coose's killer and freeing Conway. I pushed it to the back of my mind.

"We shouldn't walk far," the bounty hunter explains. My walking is stiff as I am still sore in more places than I'll admit. It warms my heart to hear his concern for me.

We pick a spot down the row of wagons and horses. There's a tree where a buggy blocks anyone wanting to spy on us. This makes me think there is more to this deal and explains the bounty hunter's silence.

"I'm sorry for David's behavior," Conway states, ever the gentleman. "Daphne is precious to us both. Anything happens to him, and well… she's his life."

I notice how he says 'us.' Does he mean because Daphne is about to marry his son, or because Conway has feelings beyond fatherly for Daphne? Either way, I bite my lip from telling him Daphne's got nuptial plans of her own. Leaving her with the gambler isn't the best idea.

"You don't have to apologize on Mr. Davenport's behalf," I say. "I didn't try to kill her. Harris would have pushed her or even shot her."

The color in his face pales slightly. "And you both ended up going down the stairs for a matter concerning neither of you. I don't feel I could have paid you enough," Conway sighs. "I don't believe your husband explained the nature of our deal with you?"

I glare over at the bounty hunter. "He hasn't told me anything."

"Mr. Conway and Mr. Davenport have agreed that instead of buying your land, they wish to purchase the right of way to lay track through the corner of your claim. It reaches the edge where the tunnel comes through the mountain."

"No," I say. Panic twists around my gut and explodes into my lungs. I shake my head.

"Wait a minute," the bounty hunter is in front of me, his hands on my arms. The warmth comes through the fabric of my jacket as I can't seem to shake the chill seeping beyond my flesh. "Listen to what we're saying. You'd keep your land. You'd receive a lump sum deposited in the bank, an account set up in your name, and never need anything again. Your claim is an enormous chunk of the mountain where the tunnel goes through and comes out."

My father always said he got the land in our claim dirt cheap because no other prospector wanted a place as steep or off-putting as ours. Too bad Earl wasn't around to see the value he stumbled upon.

"No," I say again.

"There is the matter of a few details we will need to finish negotiating," Mr. Conway says. "A certain area where we would keep it reserved and off-limits." He looks at me, and my body about seizes.

"Excuse us for a moment." Grabbing the bounty hunter, I yank him to the other side of the tree. "We had a deal. No deal!" I whisper fiercely.

The bounty hunter looks me straight in the eye. "This is the best way to protect your secret, Dimples. Conway knows. There have been reports of a few natives around the railroad camp. I told him the area known as Standing Rock is off-limits. As long as they respect it, the natives will let them alone."

"You told them about Tail Feathers?"

He shakes his head. "All we need to do is ride up there, you talk to them, let them know the rail is passing through, and be civil, then all is well."

"Are you crazy!" I hiss. "They aren't going to respect the boundaries. There will be a war breaking out for sure."

My body seizes again, and the bounty hunter wraps his arms around me. "There is not going to be a war. I'll make sure of it."

"How are you going to do that?"

"I'm going to scout for them, but only until they leave the mountains, and by then, they should have enough time to find another to take them further."

"You'd do that for me?"

"I'm doing it to keep a war from breaking out," he says. "Jo, the railroad is coming through one way or another. I don't think there is any other way to protect your friends."

They're more than friends. They're family.

Looking back into those grey eyes, I agree.

Lord, please don't make me regret this decision.

Now that my claim is secure and Chitto and his tribe are safe, what's a cowgirl to do?

WHAT'S NEXT?

Give a girl a penny, a pony, and a town to defend... and she'll chase a bunch of outlaws.

When a gang of outlaws rob Deadwood's bank leaving behind a dead body, the entire town is broke. With the Sheriff out of commission and the bounty hunter on the trail, it's up to Jo to find the killer and return the cash before the whole town finds themselves drowning in more than debt.

Watch out bad guys, Jolene Willow Dean always gets her man!

ABOUT THE AUTHOR

Growing up on a farm in Pennsylvania, Susan Lower yearned for adventure. A woodsy gal, Susan prefers camping over going to the beach any day. Still a farm girl at heart, Susan writes fast action reads filled with cowboys, heroes, and hope. She writes both western historical and contemporary romances, romantic suspense, and has been itching to one day write a mystery or thriller. Christmas is her favorite holiday, and she loves to write resilient characters struggling to overcome the complications of life while holding their values and strengthening their faith.

ALSO BY SUSAN LOWER

Cowgirl Mysteries

Ever since Jo Dean came down off her mountain, she's been stuck in Deadwood trying to protect her claim and her heart. With both the bounty hunter and the gambler vying for both, how is a cowgirl to choose?

The Cowgirl Gets The Bad Guy

The Cowgirl Takes The Bounty

Silver Wind Equine Rescue Series

Love horses, cowboys, and second chances? The Silver Wind Horse Rescue series has both! While the members of the Silver Wind Horse Rescue set out to provide refuge for abused and abandoned horses, those very horses may be the salvation they need to find a second chance at love.

Forgotten Reins

Unbridled

Silver Stirrups

Hearts of Hidden Hills

Sweet and wholesome small town love stories filled with second chances and healing families provide a wonderful, feel-good read.

Residence of Her Heart

Salvaged Hearts

Reckless Hearts

Brides of Annie's Creek

Travel back to the old west where these women take love into their own hands and learn somethings can't be rushed.

Fruit Cake Bride

Thimble Bride

Postage Stamp Bride